W9-BYJ-435

Autumn Encore

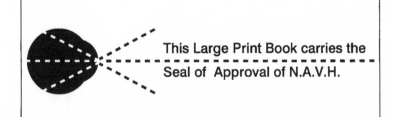

Autumn Encore*

Jane Peart

Thorndike Press • Waterville, Maine

Published in 2002 by arrangement with
Natasha Kern Literary Agency, Inc.

Thorndike Press Large Print Christian Fiction Series.

The tree indicium is a trademark of Thorndike Press.

The text of this Large Print edition is unabridged.
Other aspects of the book may vary from the original edition.

Set in 16 pt. Plantin by Myrna S. Raven.

Printed in the United States on permanent paper.

Library of Congress Cataloging-in-Publication Data

Peart, Jane.
    Autumn encore / Jane Peart.
      p. cm. — (International romance series)
    ISBN 0-7862-4638-3 (lg. print : hc : alk. paper)
    1. Pianists — Fiction.   2. First loves — Fiction.
   3. Large type books. I. Title.
   PS3566.E238 A94 2002
    813'.54—dc21   2002028616

To CRP
For creative criticism and
insightful suggestions.
"To everything there is a season,
A time for every purpose under heaven."
Ecclesiastes 3:1

Chapter One

"Nothing like starting out the year with a crisis, Mrs. Winslow," declared Dean Craddock, head of Everett College's Cultural Arts Program. "Not that it's anything *you* can't handle!"

September sunlight streaming in the office windows sent gold lights shimmering through the young widow's dark russet hair as she raised her head in surprise, the violet-blue eyes widening. The pen she held paused over the notepad in her lap. As official hostess of the college's guest residence for visiting artists and lecturers, she was accustomed to schedule changes, but she had not expected one this early in the fall term.

"Well, thanks for the vote of confidence," she smiled, "but what's the bad news?"

"I know it's a nuisance, but I'm sure you'll take it in your usual stride. Just this morning we heard from Madame Romani's manager that she has a severe throat infection and will have to cancel her concert next week. But the good news is — by an incredible stroke of luck an equally outstanding artist is available to fill in for her."

Quickly Ardith jotted down a memo to stop the greenhouse's delivery of the singer's favorite yellow roses and to have the maids remove the pink towels from the star's bedroom. Then she looked up and asked, "Who will be replacing her?"

"A gifted pianist! Luckily he has just returned from vacation in the Bahamas and won't be starting his nationwide tour for a few weeks. So his agent made the commitment for him." Dean Craddock beamed triumphantly. "It's Gavin Parrish!"

Ardith's hand jerked as her fingers tightened convulsively around her pen. Her throat went dry and her heart leaped wildly.

"Gavin Parrish?" she repeated numbly.

"Right!" Dean Craddock nodded. "Quite a coup for a small college like Everett. He's become enormously popular in the last few years, booked months ahead for concerts and —"

His words were cut off by the shrill buzz of the intercom, and he reached for the phone without finishing. He didn't see that the color had drained almost completely from Ardith's oval face, that her sweetly curved mouth was anxiously compressed, and a sudden haunted glaze darkened her extraordinarily beautiful eyes.

For a terrible moment Ardith felt as though she might faint. Struggling to hold on to reality, she looked past Dean Craddock and out the windows at the serenity of the Everett campus in the first magical transformation of fall. Flashes of crimson and ocher laced the dark evergreens and cedars along the curving road that wound through the rolling acres of velvety green lawns. Beyond, a rim of purple mountains loomed against a hazy blue sky and surrounded the peaceful North Carolina valley that underlay the historic college.

She focused on the plaque on the wall over Dean Craddock's desk, reciting to herself the words engraved on the brass: "Everett College, Founded as an Institution for the Higher Education of Young Women in 1847." Concentrating, she repeated them over and over, trying somehow to insulate herself from shock. Dean Craddock's call promised to be lengthy, and like a drowning person clutching at a straw, Ardith grasped at the moment to regain her composure. She got up, walked over to the window, and gazed with unseeing eyes out over the peaceful campus. Students and faculty members strolled by in the glorious sunshine of the fall morning as if nothing had happened, as if her whole life had not just crashed into a thousand pieces.

Gavin Parrish. Gavin! Coming here!

A deep shudder shook her, and she hugged herself with her arms to keep from shaking visibly.

She tried to focus on the scene in front of her. Just beyond the well-kept, rolling, velvety green lawns and the yellow brick buildings, a ring of maples tinted with the first flame of autumn bordered the road around the college. But Ardith could not really see the brilliant beauty of the October day. Superimposed upon the background of Everett's campus was a face fixed indelibly upon her memory, no matter how hard she tried to erase it. It was a thin, sensitive face, with dark brooding eyes, tousled black hair falling over a broad forehead, and a full, expressive mouth — the mouth that had covered hers with kisses of intense, youthful passion — Gavin!

Even when she closed her eyes she could see the impatient way he had of tossing back that errant lock of hair, the smile that suddenly lifted the melancholy from the depths of those burning coal eyes. Gavin! How she had loved him — the feel of his arms around her, the soft, warm sweetness of his lips searching out her quick, willing response.

Ardith shivered in the warm sunshine. Then Dean Craddock's voice broke in upon her memories of a long-ago time, and she turned back into the room.

"I'm afraid we'll have to postpone our discussion for now, Mrs. Winslow. Something else has come up. Perhaps we can meet again later this afternoon — say, about four? Then we can go over the arrangements for meeting Mr. Parrish at the airport."

"Of course." Ardith was surprised at the steadiness of her reply. She gestured to the French doors leading out to the terrace. "I'll just leave through the garden. Call me at your convenience."

Once outside, Ardith paused uncertainly. She felt decidedly shaky. Before she met anyone or had to deal with anything more, she needed time.

As she walked across campus, she was greeted by students and faculty members alike. But, as usual, she was unaware of the approval in their glances that her slim figure and distinctive style always evoked.

At twenty-eight, Ardith was a pretty young woman who had touched the college campus with poise and grace.

Dazedly, she found her way into the walled garden behind the college chapel and onto a stone bench beside a fountain. She could sit for a while without being interrupted in the still and deserted garden, fragrant with top-heavy late roses.

She had discovered this place when she first came to Everett and Bower House as the youngest person ever hired for her position. When she was overwhelmed by its challenges and responsibilities, Ardith found this recessed garden a perfect retreat for prayer and meditation. Here also was a sanctuary from an emotionally burdening past.

At twenty-five she had hoped to put the past behind her forever, to make a new life for herself. Her marriage had ended in a shocking accident that left her a widow, not grieving but guilty — guilty because she had never loved her husband Tedo Winslow. And she had not loved him because she had never stopped loving Gavin Parrish.

In these three years she had found a hard-won peace free of the trauma of the past. Now by some strange twist of fate,

Gavin Parrish, whom she had tried desperately to forget, was suddenly coming into her life again. *Gavin!* Ardith clenched her hands. *After all this time!*

Ten years ago seemed like yesterday.

On a June day in New York harbor, a huge luxury liner made ready to set sail for Europe with laughter, shouts, and tangles of confetti streamers surrounding a group of young people embarking on a summer tour. Ardith had just turned eighteen, and the trip was a gift from her stepfather and mother upon her graduation from boarding school.

All the gaiety and excitement of the bon voyage party came back, the thrill of being on her own — even on such a well-chaperoned trip. The second day out she had met Gavin. Twenty-six years old, he was not among the carefree college boys on board for a summer of fun and travel. Instead, he was with his teacher, Hans Friedborg, and was on his way to perform in an international competition in Vienna.

They had met the second day out, and by the third day of the five-day trip they were in love. It was the first love for either of them, and they were stunned by the sheer joy of being together.

Escaping Hans' watchful eye and thereby Gavin's practice schedule became a game to them. During the crossing they took every opportunity to meet for a few stolen hours.

They were thrilled to discover they would both be in Switzerland at the same time. While Hans was visiting relatives there, Gavin would have some time on his own. Since Ardith would be staying in Zurich with her tour, they quickly devised plans to meet.

With some deft arrangements and the connivance of a roommate, Ardith managed to slip away from the planned tour and meet Gavin in a nearby village a short train ride from the city. He met her at the little station, and they laughed and hugged each other excitedly, exuberant at their own cleverness.

Switzerland was magic. It looked just the way it was supposed to. It was a picture postcard country of music-box houses, flowers spilling out of window boxes, cobblestone streets, and rosy-cheeked children. Everything seemed special as they wandered hand in hand along the flower-bordered streets of the small town, browsing in shops, eating pastries outside under the trees in a brick courtyard of a chalet, watching sturdy mountain climbers in lederhosen and alpine hats go by with their knapsacks. The air was crystal clear; the sky, a blue umbrella. Spiky snow-topped mountains were reflected in a sapphire lake in front of the hotel.

That was the day of their picnic, the day the plans and promises were made. That was the day of the kisses, the vows of forever, the sweet excitement of their future — a future they would spend together. That was the day they had exchanged the Mizpah coin, two halves dividing the ancient prayer, "The Lord watch between me and thee while we are absent one from another."

"It will only be six weeks!" they kept reassuring each other.

Back at the hotel, they kissed long and ardently, parting only until the following day when he saw her off with her tour group at the train station before he rejoined Hans in Basel. Then he went on to the competition in Austria.

For Ardith, newly and ecstatically in love, the rest of Europe — the cathedrals, the castles, even the catacombs — passed in a montage. She moved through the tour in a daze of one hotel room after the other, always dreaming of Paris in September when she and Gavin would be reunited.

That September, at a sidewalk café in Paris, an eighteen-year-old girl sat alone at a table waiting for her beloved as the shadows grew long and the afternoon turned cold. She waited in vain, for he never came.

Ardith returned home irrevocably changed from the lighthearted girl who had left in June.

Late that September she enrolled in a prestigious New England college, where she arrived with trunk-loads of cashmere sweaters, designer jeans, leather bags and boots, and a fur coat. Outwardly she seemed the same, a vibrant sparkling beauty, destined to attract plenty of admirers. But as the New England fall slowly turned into a frozen winter, something in Ardith froze, too. For months she had waited in anguished hope for some word from Gavin — a letter, a phone call, even a postcard — some explanation. As time went by, she changed. Wearily she dragged herself to classes, but she turned down invitations, shunned social activities, avoided friends.

Gradually her hope drained away and she lost all heart. She neglected a stubborn cold until the college physician recom-

16

mended a long recuperation at home. At her mother and stepfather's new villa in Florida, she met "Tedo," Theodore Stanton Winslow II, scion of a wealthy real-estate family.

Intrigued by her mysterious melancholy and fragile beauty, Tedo pursued her stubbornly. Finally, in a desperate gamble that he might make her forget Gavin, Ardith agreed to marry him.

They were married on the Spanish-style patio of her mother's new house by a local judge. At the reception Ardith knew hardly anyone. They were all her stepfather's business acquaintances, her mother's bridge club members, the Winslows' friends. There was champagne, imported caviar, a Mexican band, and dancing, the sun dazzling the whole time on the aqua-tiled swimming pool. Ardith, feeling dizzy and dazed, wanted to run away. It all seemed like something out of a dream or — as it turned out — a nightmare.

Almost from its beginning, Ardith knew her marriage was a terrible mistake. How could it succeed when she was still in love with Gavin Parrish?

But that in itself was not the only cause of its failure. She had married a handsome playboy, a selfish and reckless weakling spoiled by his wealthy mother. Ardith soon found he was easily bored and craved constant attention, incessant activity, and round-the-clock companionship. She had nothing in common with his friends and disliked the frequent parties that lasted until three in the morning.

Ardith drew a long, shaky breath, returning to the present with an unpleasant jolt. Paris had come and gone ten years ago. She had not followed Gavin's career, never had given in to the temptation to attend a concert, not even when he had played in Washington, D.C., or somewhere she could have easily arranged to go. She had not bought any of his albums or tapes. Gradually the possibility of ever seeing him again had faded. It was all gone — or had been until today.

Ardith did not know how long she had been sitting in the garden. She gradually became conscious of the sound of the water playing lightly in the fountain nearby, and in the distance the campus clock struck noon.

Slowly she came to a decision. She would no longer let Paris poison her life. She had come too far for that. *God help me!* she prayed silently, *I won't let myself be*

18

drawn into an emotional whirlpool again! With God's help she had survived before, and with him by her side she would survive again.

She thought of the Scripture she had read in the first chapter of Joshua only that morning: "I will not leave you nor forsake you." In her early heartbreak, her illness and depression, even the despair that had followed Tedo's accidental death, God had carried her when she could not walk alone.

Ardith straightened her slender shoulders, stood up, and then started walking toward Bower House. The mere routine of her duties as college hostess would see her through until Gavin's arrival.

After that — well, she would trust God's promise.

Chapter Two

The week passed with incredible speed. Suddenly it was Thursday, the day of Gavin's scheduled arrival.

Ardith awoke early from a night of fitful sleep and troubled dreams. She was distracted during her prayer time.

Turning the pages in her Bible randomly, which she seldom did, Ardith came across a verse in the first chapter of Joshua: "Be strong and of good courage; do not be afraid, or be dismayed, for the Lord your God is with you wherever you go."

Even to the airport to meet the man whom she had once loved with all her heart and lost?

She had refrained from making a big deal about what she wore. But as she started to dress she was immobilized by indecision. *What difference does it make?* she asked herself scornfully. But she knew it did make a difference how Gavin first saw her after ten years.

Ten years made an enormous difference. Change was inevitable. Ardith scrutinized herself in the mirror. Her face had lost its youthful roundness, but her skin, still lightly tanned from her summer at the beach, was smooth except for a few tiny lines around her eyes. Her figure was youthfully slender, if slightly thinner than it was at eighteen. Maybe Gavin wouldn't even recognize her. Maybe he had forgotten all about her! Ardith frowned at her image in derision. Annoyed with her self-preoccupation, she pulled a three-year-old suit of soft tweed from her closet, knowing its color was becoming. Telling herself it didn't matter how Gavin saw her was a lie! It did matter. It mattered terribly.

In a way it had been a relief when, at the last minute, Paul Glenn, the head of Everett's music department, had decided to accompany her to meet the famous Gavin Parrish. It had eased her own nervous anxiety.

Ever since she had heard that Gavin was coming, she had felt moments of sheer panic, moments when she had wanted to run from the inevitable confrontation with her past, moments of dreading that first eye contact. If she could have escaped this meeting, Ardith would gladly have done so. But of course it was impossible. She had not even been able to bring herself to mention casually that she had known Gavin long ago.

She was glad of Paul's monologue on the way to the airport. He was excited actually to be meeting Gavin Parrish after admiring him for years. His chatter relieved her of the effort of making conversation and even lessened her own tension. All Ardith had to do was nod or answer in monosyllables.

The small airport teemed with activity. The incoming flight was one of four daily, and it was a turnaround, which boarded northbound passengers as soon as the southbound passengers deplaned. People stood in long lines at the ticket counter.

Gavin's flight arrival was announced on the PA system.

Ardith's heart began thundering. Every nerve tensed as Paul took her arm and herded her toward the entrance marked "Arrivals." And then she saw him towering over the other passengers coming down the plane's steps. There was no mistaking him. She would have known Gavin anywhere.

He paused, looking about as he entered the main lobby. Paul Glenn rushed forward, and Ardith waited, taking a deep breath and the opportunity to observe him before he saw her.

He was tanned to a handsome bronze, probably from his recent vacation in the

Bahamas. The first thing she noticed was that the vulnerability was gone from his expression, replaced by the assurance of a man used to being catered to and served. The high-bridged nose seemed more suited to his matured face than it had been to his lean, boyish one. But his deep-set eyes still seemed to have a restless, searching look.

Then suddenly as his glance swept the lobby, his eyes locked with hers. There was an instant of shocked recognition. For that moment, the noise and bustle of the busy airport swirled around them unheeded, as if they alone existed.

But before she could move or speak, Paul grabbed Gavin's hand, pumping it enthusiastically and declaring in an unnecessarily loud voice, "Mr. Parrish, Paul Glenn here, professor of music at Everett College. We're so proud to have you. Welcome."

Gavin's eyes barely grazed the small, balding man. Instead they moved over his head to where Ardith stood. The look on his face conveyed undisguised disbelief.

As the two men moved slowly toward her, Ardith's legs trembled, and she wondered vaguely if she would collapse. A cold, sick feeling moved over her as might a chill wind off a winter sea. Gavin's eyes regarded her coldly. His unmasked surprise froze into set guardedness.

She steeled herself as Paul made the introductions that only she and Gavin knew were unnecessary.

"And this is Mrs. Winslow, our official hostess at Everett, who will see to your needs during your stay."

Ardith's body stiffened. She managed a faint smile, a nod. Gavin's eyes were riveted on her face. He made a slight continental bow. *How unlike the awkward boy from the Midwest,* she thought. But of course now he was a celebrated pianist, a worldly cosmopolitan.

"Mrs. Winslow," Gavin repeated slowly, and the icy coldness of those two words chilled Ardith. He ignored her extended hand, and she withdrew it quickly, feeling his rebuff.

"While you're at Bower House, Mr. Parrish, Mrs. Winslow will be your hostess."

"Really?" Gavin's eyebrows lifted, but his eyes never left Ardith.

She felt her cheeks grow warm under Gavin's relentless scrutiny.

"Yes, indeed, your every wish will be her command. Right, Ardith?" Paul blundered on jovially. He held out his upturned palm to Gavin, offering, "If you'll give me your claim checks, I'll see about getting your luggage." Then he slipped away into the crowd.

Gavin looked piercingly at Ardith. "Mrs. Winslow! And *who* is the fortunate Mr. Winslow and *where* is he? And how long have you been married, and what in the world are you doing *here?*" He seemed to be as bewildered as he was hostile.

Ardith moistened her lips and started to answer, to try to explain, but before she could speak, they were interrupted.

"Excuse me, Mr. Parrish. I'm Susan Graham from the Everett *Times-Courier.* Could we have a moment for a quick interview, some pictures?" The woman had pushed in front of Ardith, forcing her to step aside. A young man with a camera was right behind her.

Ardith watched as Gavin graciously submitted to what must have been a repetitious ordeal of small-town reporters' basic questions. He stood stoically when a couple of flashbulbs fizzled, then posed again.

By this time Paul had returned with Gavin's handsome leather suitcase.

"Come along," he spoke to Gavin. "In an airport this small we've got no parking

25

problems. My car's right outside. I guess that's a lot different from the international terminals you're used to, right, Mr. Parrish?"

Ardith and Gavin followed, Gavin holding the glass door of the terminal exit for her with an elaborate courtesy that made her feel still more uncomfortable.

In the parking lot Paul unlocked the station wagon and went around to stow Gavin's bag in the back. Gavin opened the car door and motioned Ardith into the front seat. She hesitated, casting a hopeful glance at the roomy back seat.

"I can sit in the back," she murmured.

"Don't be ridiculous," Gavin said curtly.

Not wanting to make an issue of it, she slid into the front seat beside Paul at the driver's wheel, and Gavin got in beside her. His nearness caused her heart to trip crazily. He put his arm along the edge of the seat behind her, and automatically she leaned forward, then felt the chill of his withering glance.

Fortunately the drive from the airport to Everett College took less than half an hour. Even so it seemed too long to Ardith who was in a frenzy of indecision and tension. What kind of a game was Gavin playing? She tried to think of ways to mention casually that they had known each other before. But the thought of bringing it up was too painful, and she could not.

Fortunately, Paul kept up a running conversation as they drove, pointing out points of local interest, mentioning bits of the town's history.

"This county signed the Declaration of Independence a full year before the rest of the colonies," he commented as they were going past the stately old courthouse.

"Maybe that's what I remembered when my agent called me about filling in for Madame Romani." Only Ardith caught the heavy sarcasm in Gavin's reply. "I knew there was something familiar about this place. I was sure I'd heard of it somewhere, sometime, long ago. I think it must have been my curiosity that motivated me to accept this concert on such short notice.

"In fact, I cut short my vacation to come. There was something about the name Everett, North Carolina, that nagged at me. In the end, I knew I had to come see for myself."

Every word was a stiletto thrust into Ardith's heart. She had told him about the town where she had grown up, about its beautiful springs and falls, about how the Swiss mountains reminded her of North

Carolina. Gavin had wanted to know everything about her. Now she knew he remembered it all, remembered it well.

As they turned into the stone gates leading onto the Everett College campus, Ardith stared straight ahead, not daring to look at Gavin.

The campus looked beautiful now in the autumn morning sunshine, its rolling acres flawlessly tended and the flowerbeds brilliant with fall blossoms. Newer buildings blended harmoniously with the yellow brick of older ones, all in the same eighteenth-century architecture.

"We'll drop Mrs. Winslow off at Bower House," Paul said. "Then I can take you over to the administration building to meet Dean Craddock. From there we'll go right to the auditorium so you can supervise the placing of the piano and test the acoustics. We're due to have lunch in the faculty dining room at one. Tonight after the concert there's a reception for the faculty members and their spouses and the senior music majors at Bower House. Of course I'll bring you back there in plenty of time for you to rest and eat before your performance —"

"I never eat before a performance," Gavin said bluntly. "Just something light —"

"I'm sure Mrs. Winslow can arrange whatever you want. Right Ardith?"

"Of course."

They turned into the little lane at the south end of the campus and stopped in front of a pink brick Georgian house nestled under lovely old elms.

"Here we are," Paul announced, and Gavin got out and held the door open for Ardith. As he put out his hand to help her, and as his strong, supple, square-tipped fingers closed over her smaller ones, an electricity passed between them. He held her hand a little longer than necessary.

As she tugged gently to remove it from his grasp, Ardith struggled to steady herself. She asked him, as if he were any other guest, "What time would you like to be served?"

"Let's see. The concert is at eight, isn't it? Six would be fine. But I don't want much, something very light."

"I'll leave the order with the housekeeper, then, for a tray brought to your room a little before six. Fruit, cheese, crackers?"

"Oh, and —" Gavin began, then stopped. A strange, little knowing smile touched his mouth as he went on, "You wouldn't possibly have any goat's milk, would you?"

"Goat's milk?" she echoed blankly.

"Yes, you know like in *Heidi*."

Ardith's face flamed. Of course, he did remember! The picnic in the Swiss meadow! He was flinging her own words back at her to be sure she knew he remembered their last golden day together. They had taken a lunch and climbed to that alpine hillside. Ardith had laughingly remarked, "Just like Peter and Heidi. All we need is goat's milk."

"Well, never mind. It was only a whim," Gavin said smoothly, his cold eyes not missing her reaction. He shrugged indifferently. "It was a passing fancy, actually, for something I remembered — I'm sure you've had such yourself."

With that he gave her another continental bow and got back in the car with Paul. They drove off.

Ardith, her hands clenched into tight fists, watched them disappear around the curve of the driveway. Then she turned slowly and stiffly mounted the shallow stone steps into the house.

As soon as she had stepped across its threshold Ardith experienced the sense of sanctuary she always felt in Bower House.

It had been the home of Sara Everett Bower, a descendant of the college's founder, who had willed it and its furnishings to the school to be used as a guest residence.

Inside, all was quiet elegance. The drawing room and dining room were furnished with priceless antiques. China cabinets held complete sets of Sèvres and Wedgwood; the Sheraton buffet, drawers of sterling-silver flatware. The floor-to-ceiling bookshelves in the library were lined with rare books, some first editions and classics. The floors were covered with Oriental rugs; the windows, hung with satin draperies.

At the back of the house Ardith had a private apartment. She hurried past the more ornate rooms down the wide center hall, seeking a chance to be alone and recover from the emotional turmoil of her first encounter with Gavin.

She closed the apartment door behind her and leaned against it thankfully, already beginning to feel the comforting serenity of her surroundings. Here were all her favorite things — some from Sunnyfields where her grandmother Charlotte still lived. Other pieces she had collected and brought here to make the place where she spent nine months of each year truly her own.

The small living room was filled with sunshine, giving the maple pieces the mellow sheen of dark honey. Bouquets of purple asters mixed with the bright oranges and yellows of calendulas were arranged in the glazed mountain pottery she had placed on the low coffee table in front of the sofa and on the knotty pine mantelpiece. Needlepoint pillows from her grandmother's nimble fingers embellished the sofa and the two easy chairs on either side of the fireplace. It was a room of charm and color, comfortable as well as comforting. Here she had found a haven from the years of troubled unhappiness.

Today she needed its soothing atmosphere.

She sat down on the sofa and leaned her head back against the cushions. All she had to do was get through the next twenty-four hours, and then Gavin would be gone. He'd be out of her life as completely as he had been for ten years.

Her eyes fell on her Bible on the coffee table, still open to Joshua 1:9. "Be strong and of good courage; do not be afraid, nor be dismayed, for the Lord your God is with you wherever you go."

Ardith believed the passage had helped her through her encounter with Gavin. She closed her eyes. "Thank you, God!" she whispered. She knew now that whatever she had to go through, the Lord would be with her.

She could not let Gavin Parrish disrupt her life again! She would not. She was no longer that vulnerable girl susceptible to a romantic dream. She was a woman, strengthened by God's grace to withstand not only the past but whatever was ahead.

As Ardith dressed for the concert that evening, she was pale with excitement, and her hands shook as she fastened in pearl post earrings. They had been her grandmother Charlotte's earrings, as had the matinee-length pearls she clasped around her neck. The draped bodice, long, straight sleeves, and softly flared skirt of her claret-colored velvet dress enhanced her slender figure.

She started to close the jewel box on the dressing table when a dark green glitter caught her eyes. At the bottom of the velvet depths lay the square-cut emerald engagement ring from Tedo, who had casually dropped its sparkling weight into her palm as if it had been a trinket from a Cracker Jacks box. Emeralds had meant nothing to him nor — as she soon discovered — had their wedding vows.

Her hands on the lid, she began to shut the box again when something else caught her attention. Her fingers closed around a metallic half-circle with a jagged edge. She lifted it, then opened her palm. The sight of it wrenched her heart. It was her half of the Mizpah coin. Sudden tears blurred the engravings as Ardith read, "The Lord watch between me and thee while we are absent one from another." *Did Gavin keep his half?* she wondered. Why had *she* kept hers all these years when it only reminded her of betrayal?

Impatient with herself, she shrugged. All that mattered was getting through this evening.

Ardith flung over her shoulders the Spanish shawl her mother had given her that was lavishly embroidered with plum, peacock blue, and deep violet designs. Then she picked up the small, velvet clutch bag that matched her dress and went out of her apartment.

She wanted to check with Mrs. Lyle to see if everything was ready for the reception. She stopped at the doorway of the dining room and saw with satisfaction that Mrs. Lyle might have been prepared to entertain royalty. Everything was in exquisite order. The table had been extended to its full length. Its polished mahogany surface reflected the ornate silver epergne holding golden pears, scarlet apples, and purple grapes, all spilling artistically from its sculptured cups. Tall ivory candles in twisted candelabra were waiting to be lighted on the Sheraton sideboard where rows of sparkling crystal glasses and two silver champagne buckets stood. At either end of the table were silver tea and coffee services as well.

With a word of appreciation to the housekeeper, Ardith stepped out onto the porch into the sapphire blue darkness of the early autumn evening.

As she neared the auditorium, there were already two lines of people waiting for the doors to open: faculty members, students, season-ticket holders from the town. Ardith waited in the shadows until most of the crowd had entered. She had already decided she would sit alone in case her emotions betrayed her under the influence of the music. Just as Gavin appeared on the stage, she slipped in a side door and found an aisle seat near the exit.

Self-possessed and handsome in tails and white tie, he captured the audience at once. He bowed, took his place at the piano, and began to play. In the first compelling chords he captivated his listeners, and soon he had captivated Ardith as well. She was powerless against the sweeping passion, the beauty and intensity of Gavin's music. She sat through the intermission, still spellbound, and was jolted back to reality only by the audience's applause demanding more. After playing two more pieces Gavin took his bows to a standing ovation.

Why had Gavin chosen those two pieces for an encore? Beethoven's "Apassionata" and Debussy's "Claire de Lune"? The lingering melodies were unrelenting ghosts haunting her uneasy heart. The last time she had heard him play them was to an audience of one, herself in the ship's empty salon ten years before.

He had told her then, "Whenever I play this, I'll think of us, of today. There will never be another day like today, never another love like ours."

She had lifted both his hands from the piano keys and very softly kissed each finger.

Ardith drew a shuddering breath and rushed out the side door into the night air. There was still the reception to get through, and somehow she would endure it.

She had just a few minutes to compose herself before the enthusiastic concert crowd began flowing through the double front door of Bower House and milling about the rooms. Soon the drawing room, the library, and the hallway, as well as the dining room, buzzed with conversation. Even though the reception had been limited to the faculty members, their spouses, and students who were music majors, the house seemed filled with people.

Ardith moved with grace among the groups, pausing to greet here, stopping to chat there. She responded automatically to the comments about Gavin and the concert. "Yes, marvelous." "A superb craftsman." "A fine program." "A real treat for the college." "Yes, we are fortunate he was free to come."

There was a small flutter of excitement when Gavin himself arrived, escorted proudly by the dean and Paul Glenn. The usually sedate faculty group made a little rush to surround him.

Ardith turned in that direction by reflex, and over the heads of the people gathered about him, Gavin's unrelenting gaze met hers. Instinctively one hand went to her throat as if she were choking. Color rose in her cheeks, then drained. An amused half-smile touched Gavin's mouth. Then he very deliberately turned away to speak to someone, leaving Ardith weak and resentful.

Never had a reception seemed so long. Ardith found herself anxious for it to end, yet dreading the time she would be left alone with the guest of the college. Suddenly her duty as the official hostess seemed something to be escaped.

Of course she knew there would be no escape. She could not avoid Gavin indefinitely. His brooding, angry eyes followed her all evening as she moved among the guests.

After receptions at Bower House, guests were offered the option of relaxing any way they chose. Some unwound by going immediately to the guest room to bathe, read, or watch television by themselves. Others, too stimulated by the evening, preferred company, and often Ardith would sit and talk with them while they had a light refreshment.

The last thing Ardith wanted, however, was to be with Gavin in an intimate atmosphere. Perhaps if she prepared a tray to be taken to his room and pretended it was the accepted routine. . . . It was worth a try, and taking a quick glance around the drawing room, Ardith slipped out and down the hall into the pantry.

She could still hear voices as she hurriedly spread a silver tray with a linen cloth, fixed a Thermos of hot chocolate, and placed it on the tray with a plate of tiny sandwiches already stored in the refrigerator. She also put a small bowl of tea bags, a sugar bowl, and a creamer on the tray. She was just adding the appropriate silver when she suddenly became aware that the house had become quiet — too quiet.

She stood quite still, straining to hear voices from the front part of the house. But there were none. Then there was a slight noise behind her, and she stiffened. Next, a deep, familiar masculine voice spoke her name.

"Ardith."

She spun around, and Gavin was blocking the doorway.

Chapter Three

"Alone at last!" he said in a mocking voice.

Ardith felt her mouth go dry, her palms moisten. She leaned back against the counter, and her elbow hit the edge of the tray causing the cup to rattle. She moved jerkily aside, and Gavin saw the tray.

One eyebrow lifted, he glanced at it, then at Ardith, with an amused expression but guarded eyes. "Is that my bedtime snack?"

She swallowed and said haltingly, "Most of our guests like something before retiring —"

Gavin made an impatient gesture as if dismissing the idea. "Well, I have no intention of retiring. Not yet." His voice roughened. "Not until we've had a talk. I've waited all day for this chance to talk with you — to say nothing of the last ten years!"

Ardith motioned toward the tray. "Wouldn't you like something? Something other than —"

He came over beside her and interrupted her.

"What have you got there? Tea? That would be fine. I don't drink whiskey, brandy's too sweet, and it's too late for coffee. Unless you have Perrier?"

"Of course," Ardith said, smoothly moving away from him. She went to the refrigerator and got out a bottle of the imported sparkling water. "You will, of course, join me?" Gavin said as she opened a cabinet door to take down a glass. Her hand hesitated. Then she got another one.

"If you like," she murmured.

"I *do* like. All evening I've been told what a gracious hostess I have, so I expect to receive the full treatment accorded guests at Bower House." He paused, then added, "Company *and* conversation."

Ardith filled the glasses with ice cubes and put them on a smaller tray.

"Shall we take these into the library?" she suggested.

"After you." Gavin stepped aside and made a sweeping gesture toward the door.

A fire was still glowing in the library fireplace, and Ardith put the tray down on the coffee table between twin green velvet love seats. She deftly opened the bottles and poured the mineral water into the glasses, then handed one to Gavin. As their fingers brushed, a tremor passed through Ardith's hand in spite of her determined detachment.

Gavin took the glass and lifted it with a flourish. "To meetings too sweet to forget, to partings too painful to remember." His eyes seared her and his mouth twisted slightly. "In other words, to *us!*"

Ardith lowered her eyes, willing her hand not to shake as she raised the glass to her mouth. Its rim touched her lips, but she could not drink.

Gavin saw that immediately. "Does my toast offend you? The truth hurts, doesn't it?"

Ardith placed her glass down carefully on the coffee table. Feeling her knees tremble, she sat down, then clasped her hands tightly together in her lap. Slowly she looked up at Gavin and saw the steely glint in his eyes, the tight clench of his jaw.

"Obviously, you'd rather not be reminded of that meeting ten years ago? Nor of the parting?" His voice was harsh. "What a ruthless little flirt you were. It must have amused you to have that awkward Kansas farm boy fall in love with you and succumb to all your pampered southern-belle charms."

His tone became angrier. "Come on, tell me, how many innocent romances were there after me on your tour? In Italy, Spain, and certainly in France? There surely must have been someone else in Paris who kept you from meeting *me!*"

Involuntarily Ardith shuddered at the vivid memory of sitting at that little outdoor café until she was chilled by the oncoming evening and the realization that Gavin was not coming — would never come. Why was Gavin turning the whole terrible thing around? Accusing her? Demanding the explanation *she* should be asking of *him?*

"Gavin, you can't possibly —" As she started to speak Ardith was overcome with emotion, bewilderment.

"Oh, yes, I can possibly!" he interrupted. "I've waited ten years for some answers, and I intend to get them."

"I don't see the point —" She shook her head and stood up.

"Sit down, Ardith. You can't run away this time. By some strange twist of fate we've been brought together again. It's for a reason, if only to tie up some loose ends that have been bothering me for ten years. So, let's have it."

Ardith hesitated. She looked at the stern face of the man opposite her. This was not the Gavin she remembered. The soft mouth that had once kissed hers so tenderly was now unyielding. The eyes that had once gazed at her with love now looked at her coldly. But there was no use resisting his demand. They had to talk. She sat down again.

Gavin began to interrogate her with the sharpness of an inquisitor. "I understand you're a widow. Not a recent one, I'm told. When did you marry, and how long have you been widowed?"

"Nine years," Ardith replied quietly.

Gavin's eyebrows went up. "A year after — Switzerland — us?"

"A long year, Gavin," Ardith said distinctly. "And for your information there was no one else that summer. Not in Switzerland. No one in Italy or in Spain, certainly not in Paris. I was there in Paris — waiting to meet you, Gavin. But — where were you?"

"In September? In Paris? I was ready to meet you anywhere anytime, but then I never heard from you. Not a line! Not a letter or a postcard. Nothing!" His voice rose angrily. "After I put you on the train in Switzerland, I never heard from you again!"

Ardith gasped. "I can't believe that! I wrote you from every place our tour went! From Rome and Florence and Venice! From Madrid — wherever I could buy a

44

postcard and mail it. I sent them to the American Express office in Vienna, where you said you'd be!"

"I don't believe you! I went to check almost every day — or Hans did," Gavin retorted. "I never received anything at all from you!"

"I don't understand." Ardith shook her head in bewilderment. "I did write — truly! You must believe me."

Gavin set down his glass on the mantel. His dark brows met above the dark eyes that now pierced her with a penetrating look. "I never heard from you." His voice had a dreadful finality.

For a long moment the two of them simply stared at each other, the silence between them tingling with unspoken tension.

At last Ardith spoke again, her voice trembling. "I did write! Letters, cards! And I left a note at the Paris American Express telling you what hotel we'd be staying at in Paris and that there was a sidewalk café just around the corner and I'd be there waiting for you. The tenth of September. That afternoon. You had plenty of time to get it. Unless —" She stopped.

"Unless — someone intercepted your letter," Gavin finished for her.

"Hans!" they both gasped the name simultaneously.

Hans Friedborg, his teacher and mentor, his stern companion at the music competition, his vigilant watchdog had disapproved of their shipboard romance.

"He was always jealous of me!" Ardith said.

"Yes, I know. You or anyone who interfered with my career." Gavin ran his fingers through his thick dark hair, stunned by the truth they had uncovered.

"Hans had only one goal, my success. He lived vicariously in my career. I had to succeed for *him*. 'I will not have you distracted,' he would say over and over. He wanted me to dedicate myself totally to music. It was an obsession with him. He had wanted to be a celebrated concert pianist himself and hadn't made it, so — I was his chance, and he was determined not to let *anything* prevent it."

"Is he still with you?" Ardith asked.

"No. I had to get rid of him years ago. He became too possessive — irrational, really. But that's another story. To think, all these years — Begin at the beginning, Ardith, when you got back to the States. What then? Were you engaged to this man before you went to Europe? No, of course not. You would have told me." He frowned. "Ardith, I don't understand."

Ardith was tempted to tell Gavin the whole truth. It would be a relief to get rid of the burden she had carried so long alone. But why? He was leaving in the morning, back to his own life, a life altogether removed from her own.

"No, I didn't know him, wasn't engaged or anything when you and I met. His parents were my stepfather's friends.

"I thought you didn't want you and me to be. I decided the best way to get over you was to be with someone else, and Tedo swept me off my feet. He was handsome, rich, reckless, and told me he adored me.

"What can I say, Gavin? Now, at least we know we can't blame each other." Ardith struggled with the tears that threatened, her voice wavering.

Gavin paced the room. "It was all so unnecessary! So stupid! Did you know I didn't have your home address or anything? We were so sure we would meet in Paris, that we would spend the rest of our lives together, I never thought —"

"We were very young," Ardith said in a low, sad voice.

"The best years of our lives — wasted!" Gavin said bitterly. Ardith was slowly assimilating the same truth, and it was shattering. That someone else was responsible for what had happened to her life — all the unnecessary pain, the suffering, the eventual tragedy —

She stood up suddenly, her hands twisting.

"It's too much. I can't —" her voice broke.

Gavin crossed the room and stood before her. Close. Too close.

Instinctively Ardith moved back a step, but the sofa behind her prevented further movement.

"To think," Gavin began in a low, tense voice, "we could have —" What he left unfinished, both of them were thinking. He shook his head. "It's so unfair — so wrong — all these years without each other —"

Ardith put up her hand as if to ward off whatever else Gavin might say. "Gavin! Don't! Ten years is a long time."

"Too long," he snapped, his eyes moving over her like a caress. Then, his voice husky with wonder, he said, "You are still so lovely, Ardith. Unforgettably lovely. I was never able to forget you. Oh, I tried, in a hundred ways but —" He shrugged.

Her heart was racing, her breath was shallow. She could neither speak nor move.

Gavin riveted his gaze upon her and he

spoke very deliberately. "What happened, happened — whoever was to blame. Now that we've found each other again, it doesn't matter. Let's not be fools enough to let what we had slip through our fingers again."

Gavin put out his hand and touched her cheek with his finger, letting it trail down the curve onto her slender neck, resting it there gently. "I'm glad you never cut your hair," he said softly. Then he removed the hairpins one by one until the silky mass of rich brown waves fell over her shoulders.

He lifted the lustrous strands, letting them slide through his fingers. Then he bent his head forward and slowly kissed her. With only the slightest effort he had pulled her into his embrace. "Ardith, Ardith, dearest little love!"

She sighed. Then her arms went around his neck, and for a moment they silently held each other.

Ardith felt the release of all the years of bittersweet longing. Her thoughts spun crazily. *This can't be happening,* she thought. And yet it was!

Gavin turned his head and kissed her temple, her cheek, then her lips, and all the years apart melted away. When the kiss had ended, she leaned back, a little dazzled, and looked up at Gavin. He was smiling, and his dark eyes were sparkling. Then he laughed a full, exuberant laugh, held her in the circle of his arms, and said triumphantly, "See! It's still there. You can't deny it, Ardith. Whatever we once had is still there. It's as though we've been given another chance!"

Before she could speak, from somewhere, as if from a long way off, came the sound of a ringing telephone.

Its persistence brought Ardith back from the sensual mist in which she was floating. She stirred in Gavin's arms and told him, "The phone. I have to get it."

"Don't answer it," he urged, moving to kiss her again.

"I have to. I'm on duty until midnight. That's the phone from the main switchboard. It might be important."

Reluctantly Gavin released her.

Almost dizzily Ardith went out to the small alcove in the hall to the house phone. She picked it up.

"Yes, Bower House. Mrs. Winslow speaking."

"Long distance for Mr. Gavin Parrish."

"One moment, I'll get him." She put down the phone and took a minute to steady herself. She pressed the hold button, then spoke crisply to the switchboard.

"Transfer Mr. Parrish's call to his room in the guest wing, please. I'll have him take it there." Straightening her shoulders, Ardith walked back to the library. At the doorway she paused and saw Gavin standing staring into the glowing embers in the fireplace. Although the rush of feeling that swept over her almost weakened her resolve, she took a step into the room and spoke. "Gavin, the call is for you. It's long distance. They've transferred it to your room."

Gavin turned toward her. His heavy brows drew into a frown. As he passed her, he paused briefly and touched her arm. "Wait for me."

She listened to the sound of his footsteps on the polished floor to the guest wing. But she did not wait. She did not dare. As soon as she was sure he had reached his room, she went swiftly in the opposite direction back to her own apartment.

Safely inside, she shoved the bolt into place, then slumped against the door. Her head throbbed, and she felt totally fatigued. It had all been too much. The whole day had been filled with tension, emotion. Then too much had been said, too much held back. She felt exposed, vulnerable, utterly drained.

Walking stiffly, she crossed the small living room and went into her bedroom. There she caught sight of herself in the dressing table mirror and was stunned.

Her face looked haunted, her eyes filled with the tragic knowledge of useless suffering. With trembling hands she pushed back the hair tumbling around her shoulders, and a deep shudder vibrated through her. The memory of her response to his kiss frightened her. She felt betrayed by her own vulnerability to a man who had broken her heart once and might do it again.

"I have to be strong," she told her image in the mirror. Gavin would be leaving tomorrow, and she could not let her heart rule her head.

Ardith picked up her brush and began brushing her hair vigorously, but a sharp rap on her apartment door startled her and she dropped it with a clatter on the glass top of the dressing table.

The knock was followed by Gavin's voice calling her name. "Ardith! I need to speak to you." She put down her hairbrush, her widened eyes staring at herself in the mirror. She had not anticipated this aggressive pursuit. She remained frozen in uncertainty when the knock came again, this time it was more demanding.

"Ardith, I have something important to tell you. Please."

She sat there a moment longer, unmoving. Then knowing that she couldn't just ignore him, she got up. After all, Gavin Parrish was the college's guest and her responsibility at Bower House.

She picked up two side combs and quickly slipped them into her hair to secure it, then hurried to the living room. Another knock came just as she reached out her hand to unlock the door. Gavin's voice, impatient now and peremptory, came again. "Ardith, I see the light, and I know you're awake. Just open the door."

Ardith knew she had acted like a frightened child, running away while he was on the phone, knew it was immature, idiotic even. But she wasn't afraid of Gavin as much as she was of her own traitorous heart.

"I'm coming!"

She slid back the lock and opened the door halfway. Holding the edge, she stood behind it and waited for Gavin to speak.

His eyes moved over her. The annoyance

and impatience on his face gradually changed to tenderness. "Why did you run away? We haven't half finished talking."

"Gavin, I'm exhausted. Too much has happened too quickly. I — what is to be gained by more talking tonight?" she protested wearily.

"A lot! Everything! Our whole lives!" He reached out, covered her hand on the door frame with his own. "Darling Ardith, we've just found each other again. Surely, you don't think I'm going to let you go?"

"Gavin, we both have separate lives now. We've both changed. You can't possibly think we can pick up where we left off all those years ago?"

"We've been given another chance. How many people get that in this life?" Before she could argue, he rushed on. "That was my agent on the phone. I usually call after a performance to say how it went and to check in, but tonight — well, tonight was different. Anyhow, I've made arrangements to stay over a few days. After I saw you, I knew I couldn't leave until we had settled something —"

Ardith began to shake her head, but he stopped her.

"Please, darling, listen. Professor Glenn asked me to hear some of his music majors play, maybe hold a question and answer session, and I agreed. Since I don't have to be at my next concert until the middle of next week, it seemed the perfect excuse to stay.

"Don't you see how important it is, Ardith? It may be the most important thing we ever do." There was a pleading note in his voice.

"Too much time has gone by, Gavin," Ardith said, and she turned her head away from him. One of the side combs slipped out, and her heavy hair loosened, covering one side of her flushed face.

She bent to retrieve it, but he knelt quickly and picked it up, then took her hand and placed the comb into it. Keeping her hand enclosed in his, he said softly, "I love your hair down. You're so lovely. Let me come in, Ardith. There's so much more we need to say to each other."

"No." Her voice sounded strangled. "No, Gavin, it's late, too late. There's no use —"

"There is, I won't let you do this, not after I've waited ten years for this chance." His hand slipped to her wrist, encircling it and gripping it tightly.

His show of strength snapped something inside of Ardith, and she lashed out at him,

"*You've* waited ten years. Well, so have I. All my letters came back *unopened!* Maybe that was your answer. Easy enough to blame Hans when he's not here to defend himself!"

Ardith's voice cracked, and she tried to pull loose from his hold, but he only tightened his grasp. Tears of frustration and pent-up emotion coursed down her cheeks, and in another moment Gavin was in the door, cradling her in his arms.

His lips against her hair, he murmured soothingly, "Darling, darling —" He sighed, rocking her gently.

His arm around her waist, he led her over to the couch, and they sat down, her head on his shoulder as he held her close.

"Ardith, you don't really believe what you just said, do you?"

She sighed heavily. "I don't know. It's all so —"

"Now, I want you to hear me out, Ardith, to listen and consider what I have to say. Now we know neither of us was to blame for what happened. For whatever reason, we've been brought back together. We have a second chance. If I hadn't been asked to step in for the sick soprano, we might never have met again. We can't let this go. Don't you see that?"

Ardith shook her head. "I don't know. We're different; we've made our own lives. We don't really know each other anymore."

"That's just it. Now we'll have the time."

"But you're going on your tour — twelve cities, I heard you say."

"Look, my darling. We have right now. We have the next few days. I'm not due in Chicago until Tuesday. That gives us the weekend plus a day. We can live a lifetime in a few days. We did once — and we can again. Please, Ardith, say you want that too."

"Is it possible? I'm not sure."

"We can try. First, we exorcise the past. I could hate Hans if I let myself. But when I remember how much he poured into me, I can begin to understand, at least a little. He was jealous of you, of anything that would take my mind off my music. So, naturally, he had to eliminate you."

Gavin clasped Ardith's hands, brought them to his lips, and kissed them. He went on, a persuasive urgency in his voice. "Please, darling, give us this time. Somehow, we both were able to survive a deception that could have wrecked and ruined our lives. But we were cheated out of ten years of knowing and loving each other. I want to know everything that happened to you in all of those lost years."

"I was a girl of eighteen when you knew me before. Now I'm a woman. You don't even know who I am, what I've become!"

"I want to know that, too," he argued, "and so much more — all the things we didn't have time to discover about each other."

After a long moment, Ardith asked, "Would you like to come with me to Sunnyfields, where I grew up, and meet my grandmother?"

Gavin's serious expression was transformed by his wide, relieved smile.

"You mean that?" His voice revealed his excitement.

Ardith nodded. "I was planning to drive up to see my grandmother this weekend. She's expecting me. I haven't seen her since the summer."

"Yes, I'd like that —"

She rose from the couch and helped Gavin to his feet. "We'll leave in the morning. I'll have some hostess duties to take care of first, but we can still get away early."

"I'm always packed. Just let me know when you're ready to go."

She walked with him to the door, but before she had pulled it open, he passed his

58

fingers through her hair once more.

"I promise I won't pressure you in any way," he said. "There will be no obligation on your part, no commitment. I just want us to have these few days. You won't be sorry."

Tired though she was, Ardith slept badly and rose early. She put on her robe and went out to the kitchen to make coffee. While waiting for the water to boil, she watched out the window as two robins hopped from branch to branch on the apple tree at the edge of the small patio. A few minutes later she heard the easy laughter of a group of kitchen workers on their way to the college dining room.

During the night it had rained, and the morning air was sweet and fragrant. In the sunlight that filtered in dancing patterns onto the blue and white formica counters, the events of the night before seemed unreal.

Gavin Parrish back in her life. Had it been wrong to invite him to Sunnyfields? Should she heed the Cassandra-like inner voice warning her against becoming involved with the worldly man Gavin had become?

No, Ardith reassured herself. Gavin himself had said they would be sensible, not mistake romantic nostalgia for mature feelings nor let idyllic memories blind them to the reality of changes. Ardith took her coffee out onto the small brick patio off the kitchen and sat down on one of the white wicker chairs cushioned with bright chintz. As she sipped her coffee, she thought over the incredible events of the last twenty-four hours and asked herself again, *Is it too late?*

Gavin did not know how deeply she had changed.

If he knew how life-transforming her spiritual awakening had been, would he understand?

After the summer Tedo died and her life took a new direction, Ardith had become a different person. She had discovered that God's way gave her a new life and peace she had never thought she could have.

Now, Gavin had come into that life disrupting everything, and Ardith was standing on a precipice.

The outcome of the weekend at Sunnyfields was impossible to predict. Only God knew what it would be.

Chapter Four

It was late afternoon when they reached Sunnyfields. They had spoken very little during the short trip, although Ardith had been keenly aware of Gavin's closeness in the forced intimacy of her small car.

After leaving the expressway they drove through a countryside of rolling hills made glorious by the colors of fall. *It's the loveliest time of the year in this part of North Carolina,* Ardith thought, seeing it afresh through Gavin's eyes. The bright blue sky behind the darker blue ridge of mountains highlighted by verdant pines and bright flashes of crimson, yellow ocher, and burnt orange made a brilliant palette of colors an artist would yearn for.

They passed a sign announcing, "Welcome to Melrose County," and Ardith turned to Gavin and said, "It won't be long now. We're almost there."

Soon they were passing meadows enclosed with white board fencing. Then Ardith turned off the two-lane country road and started up a winding driveway to a white clapboard house drowsing on the hill in the autumn sunshine.

To Ardith, the years before her European summer seemed in retrospect all sunshine, very little shadow. She could hardly remember her father, Arthur Fielding, who had died when she was four. A few faded snapshots of them together on the beach in front of the beach cottage that later became hers and a handsome boyish face in a photograph were her only visual memories of him.

But her childhood with her grandmother Charlotte at Sunnyfields, the Fielding house for generations, had been sublimely happy and secure. Judith, her beautiful young mother, had come and gone, too restless to stay in the isolated country. Only when Judith had married Curtis Barnes did Ardith go to live with Charlotte.

Ardith felt the familiar little lifting of her heart as they approached the place she loved above all others. Her heartbeat quickened. Today the man she had loved for years was here with her.

As they slowed to a stop in front of the house, a tall, silver-haired woman with an erect, slender figure stepped out onto the deep front porch and lifted her hand in a welcoming wave.

Ardith waved back and said to Gavin,

"Well, here we are. That's my grand-mother, and this is Sunnyfields!"

They went up the porch steps together, and after Ardith had kissed her grand-mother, she introduced Gavin.

"Welcome to Sunnyfields, Mr. Parrish," Mrs. Fielding said, extending her hand.

Gavin bowed slightly as he took it. "It's a privilege to meet you, Mrs. Fielding. Thank you for allowing me to come on such short notice."

"I'm always delighted when my grand-daughter brings a guest. Come along in-side. We'll have tea."

As they entered the house, the ambiance of Sunnyfields enfolded Ardith and she felt a rush of warm affection for the wonder-fully familiar sights around her. Inviting fragrances reminded her of the happy years she'd spent in her grandmother's home — the smell of lemon wax, the spicy scent of the yellow and bronze chrysanthemums on the harvest table in the hall, and the deli-cious aroma of baking bread wafting from the kitchen.

"I wasn't sure exactly what time you would leave Everett, or when you'd get here," Mrs. Fielding said, "but I thought we'd have tea now since I planned dinner for seven."

"Tea will be fine, perfect, in fact," Gavin said quickly.

"Well, then, Ardith, take Mr. Parrish into the living room and make him comfortable. I'll be right along."

"Can I help, Gran?" Ardith offered.

"No dear, everything's ready," she said as she headed for the kitchen. "I'll bring it in as soon as the tea's made."

Gavin and Ardith walked into the living room, an unpretentious room where American antiques mingled pleasantly with comfortable chintz-covered sofas and armchairs, worn braided rugs scattered on the random-board pine floors, and ancestral portraits in ornate frames on the walls.

Gavin looked around appreciatively. "What a wonderful room! It looks like everyone's idea of what 'home' should be!"

He walked over to the piano by the window where some silver-framed family photographs were displayed. He picked up one of a handsome young man in an Air Force uniform and turned to Ardith questioningly.

"My father," she told him just as her grandmother entered, pushing a small tea cart.

Mrs. Fielding seated herself in one of the wing chairs by the fireplace and began to pour fragrant orange-spice tea into pink and white Spode cups.

"Ardith, dear, please pass Mr. Parrish the nut bread. Lemon or cream, Mr. Parrish?"

Ardith watched her grandmother's graceful movements and her total ease as she conversed with Gavin. She treated him as she would any guest at Sunnyfields, without special awe at his celebrity status.

On his part, Gavin was a gracious guest, listening attentively as Ardith's grandmother told him some of the history of Sunnyfields, the home of the Fielding family for more than a hundred years.

"There are dozens of stories here — 'if the walls could only talk!' As a matter of fact, my husband's mother, who was an English war bride and came here in 1919, started to write a history of the house and the Fielding family. Strangely enough, it seems outsiders sometimes appreciate these things more than people who grow up among them."

"I know what you mean. I grew up on a family farm in Kansas, but because of my music, I left there at fifteen to study, first in St. Louis, then in Chicago and New York. I haven't been back in years. After my mother died —" Gavin paused for a second, then went on "— my two older brothers split the property. One still lives and farms there. Somehow I've lost contact with both of them over the years. My life has been — so different."

His remark hung in the air for a poignant moment before Mrs. Fielding smoothly led the conversation to another subject. For Ardith, Gavin's statement had a special significance.

Music had been Gavin's all-encompassing priority. Evidently it had meant more to him than keeping in touch with his family, his roots. Could there possibly be any place in his life for her if — the thought dangled. There were so many "ifs" to be resolved. A few days together could not bridge the chasm created by ten years of lives so separated, so different.

Ardith was pulled back into the present by her grandmother's voice. "Ardith, I've given Mr. Parrish the colonel's room overlooking the orchards. Would you show him upstairs? There's plenty of time before dinner for a rest or a shower or —"

"All right, Grandmother. Come along, Gavin," Ardith said, rising from her chair.

"It was a lovely tea, Mrs. Fielding. Thank you," Gavin said as he followed

Ardith out of the living room and up the curved staircase.

At the landing he stopped to examine four framed bridal portraits hung in a row. One was immediately recognizable as Charlotte, regal in white velvet and a pearl-beaded headband from which trailed a delicate lace veil. The one next to hers was of a smiling blond in the same gown.

"My mother, Judith, when she married my father here at Sunnyfields. She's remarried now to Curtis Barnes," Ardith explained as she noted Gavin's questioning look. She started up the next flight of steps anxious to move on, but Gavin was still looking at the pictures.

"And *you?* When you married did you wear this gown?" he asked.

"No," Ardith answered sharply. "I was married in Florida. White velvet would hardly have been appropriate."

Gavin seemed about to say something else, then thought better of it. All he said as they reached the top of the stairs was, "You look more like your grandmother than your mother."

"I take after Gran's side of the family."

She opened the door into a spacious, high-ceilinged bedroom dominated by a massive Victorian bed. Gavin, standing behind her, raised an eyebrow and stage-whispered with an amused smile, "And who is the colonel I'm displacing by sleeping in here?"

Ardith laughed. "You'll have to get used to the way Southerners talk, Gavin. The colonel was Colonel Buford Fielding of the Confederacy. I don't know why after all these years we still call this room his. Lots of other people have slept here. He lived to be in his nineties, so maybe he was the longest tenant."

"I'll try to be duly respectful," Gavin said solemnly, "and certainly not do anything to make his great-great-great-granddaughter regret she extended the hospitality of this house to me."

Ardith laughed, seeing in Gavin's eyes for the first time the mischievous twinkle of the man she remembered. It was a welcome sign.

"Well, I think you'll be comfortable. Do make yourself at home, and I'll see you later," she said, starting to leave. But Gavin grabbed her hand, held it in both of his, and spoke earnestly.

"Thank you, Ardith. Thank you for trusting me enough to bring me here."

Suddenly Ardith wanted him to see everything, all the beloved places at Sunnyfields that were a part of her when they had first met, all the things she would have shown him if she had brought him here ten years ago.

Back in her own childhood bedroom with its spool bed, flower-sprigged wallpaper, and ruffled curtains, Ardith suddenly felt lighthearted. It was almost as if she had stepped back magically to a time before heartbreak and tragedy had touched her life. Were she and Gavin really being given a second chance at happiness?

When Ardith came downstairs just before seven, she found Gavin and her grandmother in the entrance to the dining room where Mrs. Fielding was explaining the cross symbols at the corners of the doors. "They were thought to ward off evil spirits and bring good luck to the occupants," she explained with a wry smile.

She saw Ardith then and greeted her. "Well, there you are, my dear. And how lovely you look! Ardith should always wear blue, don't you agree, Mr. Parrish? It makes her eyes look like lapis lazuli."

"Grandmother!" remonstrated Ardith gently, feeling her cheeks grow warm as Gavin's eyes confirmed her grandmother's compliment. But she was secretly happy she had worn the royal blue sweater dress tonight.

"You'll have to forgive a doting grandmother, Mr. Parrish." Mrs. Fielding laughed. "Ardith is my only grandchild and I practically brought her up myself here at Sunnyfields. Come along in. We'll have a chilled glass of our own apple cider before dinner, the first of the fall crop. Our apples and cider are famous in this part of the country, Mr. Parrish. You'll find the flavor incomparable, I'm sure."

They went into the living room where the curtains were drawn against the autumn dusk and a cheerful fire was crackling in the fireplace. On the coffee table was a silver tray with three fragile goblets and a frosted pitcher glowing with a rich amber liquid.

"I think we should have a toast tonight, our guest's first time under our roof," Mrs. Fielding suggested lightly. "I remember one my father used to give." She handed each of them a graceful, tulip-shaped glass. "To good times remembered and better times to come."

Mrs. Fielding lifted her glass to each of them in turn, not realizing how apt her toast would seem to them. Ardith drank, not wanting to meet Gavin's compelling glance.

"Shall we take our glasses in to the

70

table? Dinner is ready."

They went into the dining room, soft with candlelight and the glow of polished mahogany. Gavin seated Mrs. Fielding, then held out the chair next to her for Ardith. He took the seat Mrs. Fielding indicated for him at her right. Then she spoke, "At Sunnyfields it's our custom to ask a blessing before meals, Mr. Parrish." Mrs. Fielding held out her hand to Gavin, who only hesitated slightly and took it in his own. She held Ardith's hand in her other one, and as Ardith tentatively offered hers to him, Gavin clasped it.

As his fingers enclosed her hand, Ardith felt an immediate quickening. She drew in her breath quietly, bowed her head, and closed her eyes.

Mrs. Fielding was already speaking: "Heavenly Father, may this food we are about to partake strengthen, nourish, and refresh us. We thank thee for these and all thy many blessings in the name of thy dear Son, our Lord Jesus Christ. Amen."

Ardith felt Gavin give her fingers a slight pressure before he released them.

For as long as she could remember at her grandmother's table, family members and guests alike had clasped hands, forming a loving circle to give thanks before every meal. Her grandmother had never hesitated to demonstrate her faith this way, not always knowing if those who shared her table also shared her beliefs. True to her own faith, her traditions, Charlotte Fielding was sure of her own identity. And Ardith had always longed for that same tranquility.

Dinner was simple yet delicious as always at Sunnyfields. Savory chicken was accompanied by fluffy rice, eggplant and tomato casserole with a buttery crumb topping, and hot biscuits.

Mrs. Fielding dismissed Gavin's extravagant compliments with a slight shake of her head and a smile. "It's mostly Cora's doing. My marvelous cook prepared most of it. Although —" she hesitated with a twinkle in her eyes "— even though I do say so myself, I have a light hand with biscuits. I learned all I know about cooking from Cora, however. When I came here as a bride, I had to be taught. And Cora was an excellent teacher."

"Will she be here tomorrow?" Ardith asked.

"Yes, she only comes a few days a week now. I really don't need her, and actually she's retired. She spends a lot of time with her grandchildren."

"I want Gavin to meet her." Ardith smiled, thinking fondly of the wonderful woman who had "mothered" her when she was a little girl at Sunnyfields.

"Did she teach you to cook, too?" Gavin asked Ardith teasingly.

"Well —" hedged Ardith, "I owe my best dishes to her."

They all laughed, and then Mrs. Fielding said, "Tomorrow you must show Mr. Parrish all around. In my father-in-law's time Sunnyfields was not only a place known for its hospitality but it was a working farm as well. During the Depression the family had to sell off many of the acres, and with only Ardith and me to run it, I've gradually been selling more land. But only in large segments to people I know will farm it, not subdivide it. I want to keep this part of the country rural, with producing farms, at least as long as I am able." Mrs. Fielding's voice had a determined note.

Then swiftly she changed to a lighter subject. "I'll have Cora pack you a picnic, and you can walk down to the river bed. That way Mr. Parrish can see the orchards and the vineyards. We grow our own scuppernong grapes, Mr. Parrish, a sweet, golden kind. The taste is indescribable.

They're ripening now, so you'll get to sample some.

"The weather now is so fine. But Indian summer never lasts, so these days are precious and last-chance picnics are the most fun." Mrs. Fielding could not know that her words struck a responsive chord in both her listeners, who remembered another picnic they had shared on a Swiss hillside ten years ago.

"I'd like that very much, Mrs. Fielding," Gavin said. His eyes glanced over to catch Ardith's, and she was glad the subdued light from the candle glow hid her instant blush.

"Let's take our coffee into the living room," Mrs. Fielding suggested.

"A superb dinner, Mrs. Fielding," Gavin remarked as they settled themselves in front of the flickering fire behind the brick hearth.

"That's quite a compliment from someone who has probably eaten in some of the finest European restaurants," Charlotte answered, making her first reference to Gavin's traveled life.

"I envy you your home, Mrs. Fielding, your sense of belonging. I find it hard to imagine living all one's life in the same house."

"And I envy you your talent. I have no musical ability myself except to enjoy it in others. I believe with Joseph Addison that music is 'the greatest good that mortals know, and all of heaven we have below.' "

When they had finished their coffee, Mrs. Fielding rose. "I have an early appointment in town tomorrow, so I'll say good night now. Stay and enjoy the fire as long as you like. Mr. Parrish, we have a fair library if you'd like to take a book along to bed. Come see me before you go upstairs, will you dear?" she asked Ardith before she left the room.

Gavin followed Mrs. Fielding's graceful figure with his eyes and then turned to Ardith. "You two are very much alike, you know. You both have an inner radiance and honesty, and yet you have a certain reserve that is — well, special." He shrugged as if he could not find the right words. "And, of course, you resemble each other physically a great deal."

"Oh, but Grandmother was a great beauty! And still is beautiful," Ardith asserted. "I thank you for the compliment, but I don't really think so."

Ardith could not see herself as Gavin saw her. In the firelight her face had a luminous mellow glow that softened her cheekbones, defined the lovely curve of her mouth, and accentuated the dark waves framing her delicate face.

She felt his eyes on her, and her breathing became shallow. The quickening of her pulse reflected the intensity of her feelings.

She quickly rose from the sofa. "I think I should go now, too. Good night, Gavin. Sleep well."

Before he could protest, she left the room walking quickly down the hallway to her grandmother's bedroom.

She found her reading, propped up against pillows in her high, pineapple-postered bed. She looked up from her book and over her glasses as her granddaughter sat down on the edge of the bed.

"So this is the man you met, loved, and lost long ago?" Mrs. Fielding asked her sympathetically, reaching out and covering Ardith's hand with her own slender one.

Ardith nodded. "Yes, Gran, what do you think of him?"

"I've just met him, remember. How can I tell?"

"You always have an opinion, Gran. I know you."

"Yes, but I've come to question first impressions, dear. They can be wrong so

76

often. Give me a little time to get to know your Gavin Parrish."

"Will three days be long enough? He has to leave on Sunday."

"Sometimes you can learn a lot about a person in three days. Others it takes a lifetime to know, and even then —" Her grandmother shook her head slightly. "I will tell you this much. What I saw, I liked."

"Really?" Ardith brightened.

"But whether or not he's the man for you, Ardith, that I don't know."

"Neither do I, Gran, but as I said on the phone, he is the man I would have married if — if things hadn't gone wrong for us."

"Yes, I know. Still, I believe everything happens for a purpose. Everything happens by God's will. What we do about the things that happen to us in life, that's up to us. Maybe you and Gavin were not right for each other then. Maybe you're still not right for each other. Only you can find that out."

Ardith considered her grandmother's words, knowing it would be well to take them into account. She leaned forward and lay her cheek on her grandmother's smooth one. "Thank you, Grandmother."

"For what? Unasked-for advice?" Mrs. Fielding laughed softly.

"For loving me, for just being you." She kissed her forehead. "Good night, Grandmother."

"Good night, dear. Sweet dreams!"

Later as she turned out the light in her bedroom, Ardith wondered if she could capture the joy she had once shared with Gavin.

How could she let him know how much of a difference ten years had made in her life? How could she show him how her life had changed?

She remembered that dark time in her life right after Tedo's fatal accident.

She had gone to Sunnyfields and asked her grandmother for the keys to the family beach house. Knowing Ardith was numbed by shock, her grandmother had asked Charlie Mercer, Ardith's childhood friend and their neighbor in Melrose, to drive her to Seawood Beach.

They had traveled most of the way in silence. Ardith was incapable of conversation, and Charles was compassionate and understanding, for he had loved Ardith for years.

When they had reached the cottage and he'd carried in her suitcase and box of supplies, he was reluctant to leave.

"I don't like the idea of your being here alone," he'd said.

78

"I meant to be alone, Charlie. I need to be alone," Ardith had told him firmly.

"But, it's not — I mean, you're too — too much has happened; you're too young —"

"I feel a hundred years old, Charlie, and this is something I have to work out for myself."

As it turned out, it was the best thing she could have done.

When she'd unpacked her suitcase Ardith found her grandmother had slipped in a Bible. She was touched, for she knew her grandmother had hoped she would find comfort from reading it, but her grandmother couldn't have known Ardith felt too guilty to pray.

She had married a man she didn't love, then failed him as a wife. Disappointed in his bride, Tedo had soon found others to fill her place. She had often been the target of his violent temper, and although she had become terrified and desperate, still Ardith thought she was partly at fault. Two wrongs don't make a right.

When Tedo was killed racing his speed-boat, she was consumed with the guilty knowledge of her relief to be free. She felt beyond prayer, beyond forgiveness.

For the first few days at the cottage, she had seemed incapable of feeling or thinking, much less of praying. Her oppressive weariness was as much spiritual as physical. Guilt weighed on her like a heavy stone, guilt because she could not grieve for Tedo, because she had never loved him.

Her life at the beach took on a pattern. Every day she walked for hours, then sat or lay and let the soothing combination of sand, sea, and sun work its power on her shattered nerves. At first, unable to hold a thought, she simply rested, relaxing in nature's rhythm.

Then one morning when she woke, the sun was shining. Her coffee smelled fragrant and tasted strong and delicious, and she knew life was stirring once again in her numbed body.

As she was packing her tote bag to spend a day on the beach, she spotted the Bible her grandmother had sent, and on impulse she tucked it into her bag.

Slowly, systematically she began a daily reading. At first it had had no impact. The words had seemed meaningless; the language, archaic. But determined, she read on.

One day when she was reading through the thirtieth chapter of Deuteronomy, a phrase leapt off the page and grabbed her attention.

"I have set before you life and death," she read, repeating the words aloud, "therefore choose life."

They seemed to say that she could not bury herself indefinitely in her small, isolated beach house, that she could not wallow forever in self-pity and useless regret.

An excitement of understanding ran through her as she remembered another Scripture she had read recently in the New Testament: "I am come that they may have life, and that they may have it more abundantly."

Ardith felt the warm saltiness of tears, like a spring thaw after winter, melting the cold hardness within her. Those tears were healing, washing away all her fear of the future, her guilt, her burdened heart, freeing her as she wept.

At the time she did not fully realize what had happened. All she knew was that she had consciously chosen life, life to be lived abundantly in belief in the Lord Jesus Christ. When she had been drowning, a clear, reassuring offer of life rescued her.

She turned down her mother's pleas that she come back to Florida and, instead, took an apartment near Everett College, registered for classes, and eventually got her degree. She spent a great deal of her time at Sunnyfields and every summer at the beach house. When the job at Bower House became available, Ardith applied and was accepted.

So her new life had begun.

Now that life was being shaken by the reappearance of Gavin Parrish.

Would he understand the life she had chosen for herself? Was there room in that life for him? Although her heart had awakened from a deep sleep, she knew that she could continue to live without him. But could he understand that? Could he share her new spirituality?

She was still yearning for the answers to her questions when she drifted off to a troubled sleep.

Chapter Five

When Ardith awoke, her room was full of sunshine, and she realized she had slept later than usual. The grandfather clock in the front hall was striking nine forty-five as she came running down the stairs.

Gavin came in from the porch as she reached the bottom step. "You look about twelve years old!" he greeted her, taking in her casual jeans, oversized sweater, and sneakers. Her long hair was loosely tied back by a narrow red ribbon.

"Practically my uniform at Sunnyfields," she laughed, "but you look much too dressed up for a country picnic!" She eyed his gray slacks, open-collared blue shirt, and V-necked gray sweater.

Gavin pretended chagrin. "It's all I had with me!"

"I was just kidding. Come on. Let's get some coffee."

"Sleepyhead!" he accused. "I've been up for hours. I thought we were supposed to get an early start on our picnic."

"We have to have some breakfast first. Can't hike these hills on an empty stomach."

"Empty stomach?" Gavin groaned. "Cora fixed me one of the biggest breakfasts I ever had — ham, scrambled eggs, biscuits, and *grits!* Never had them before. They're great!"

They went into the dining room where a carafe of coffee stood on an electric warmer on the buffet. Ardith poured the coffee and brought the cups to the table. There she helped herself to a biscuit from a basket and buttered it.

"Want one?" she asked Gavin.

"No thanks. I'm saving my appetite for the picnic Cora fixed us. I don't know what all she put in there, but when I tried to lift it —" He shook his head as if words failed him.

Ardith laughed. "I can imagine. I know Cora's idea of a picnic!"

There was a pause for a moment before Gavin spoke seriously. "You were lucky growing up in a home like this."

Ardith nodded. "Yes, I guess I was. But I didn't realize it until I had to leave."

"I think I missed a real childhood. After my talent for music was discovered — well, things changed drastically for me. My mother recognized it when I was about nine or ten. She wanted me to have the best teachers, so I boarded in town where I could have lessons. I think that's when I began to lose touch with my family, my home —"

The thought of Gavin as a lonely little boy moved Ardith, and impulsively she placed her hand on his arm. He looked at her quickly and covered her hand with his own.

"I'm not painting a dark picture of my growing-up years to gain sympathy, Ardith. It's just that — sometimes — I wish —" He stopped and smiled at her. "Don't look so sad, darling! It's all balanced out. Really! And today's too special to spend talking about things that can't be helped. Let's be happy!"

He leaned toward her and kissed her mouth, then sighed rapturously. "Mmmmm! Butter's my favorite flavor."

They were laughing as Mrs. Fielding entered the room, her arms full of fresh shasta daisies and some late dahlias. "What! You two haven't left for your picnic yet? You'd better get started. The sun goes down quickly behind the hills in the fall, you know, and cuts the afternoon short."

Gavin stood up. "It's your slugabed granddaughter's fault, Mrs. Fielding," he told her, pointing to Ardith with mock severity.

"I'm ready, I'm ready!" She took a final sip of coffee, then pushed back her chair.

As they picked up the hamper and walked outside, Ruff, the old collie, got to his feet from the sunny corner of the porch, wagging his plume of a tail. After Ardith paused to rub his head behind his ears, he followed them down the porch steps and as far as the pump house. Then, as if he knew they would be going farther than his legs would easily carry him, he sank down in the long grass with an audible sigh. He placed his head between his paws and watched Gavin and Ardith with tawny, sad eyes as they went through the gate to the old orchard path.

Soon they were in the woods that bordered the far meadow, walking through a grove of trees over the pine-needle–carpeted ground.

Looking up at the tall man walking beside her, Ardith was sharply reminded of another sun-dappled day when they had set out for a picnic together. Ardith's heart swelled in anxiety. Was it really possible to find what they had lost?

Almost as if he shared her thoughts, Gavin shifted the basket handle to his other side and found her hand. He looked down at her and smiled.

Instantly happiness soared within her. Maybe this was enough, all one could hope for. Maybe the present moment is all one ever has. Maybe no one should try to bring back the past.

They found a warm, sunny spot close to the wide part of the creek they had been walking alongside and spread out a blanket. Stretching out on it and folding his arms behind his head, Gavin gave a sigh of satisfaction. "Perfect!" he announced.

Ardith opened the hamper and took out a blue-checked tablecloth and lay it over the blanket. Then she brought out silver wrapped in blue-checked napkins and paper plates set into wicker holders.

"Hungry?" she asked him. Gavin looked at her for a moment, then said, "I hate to admit it after that breakfast I had, but — I am! It must be all this fresh air. I'm not used to it. I spend most of my days in musty practice studios. Besides, I'm curious to see what that paragon of gourmet cooks put in that basket!"

"Just wait until you see!" Ardith said knowingly. She unfastened the lid and began to set out the foil-wrapped cold fried chicken, buttered, sliced homemade bread, apples, pears, and frosted carrot cake. There were two Thermoses — one of lemonade, the other of coffee.

Ardith looked up suddenly to see Gavin's eyes watching her graceful movements.

"How lovely you are," he said softly, and she drew in her breath, feeling suddenly shy under Gavin's open admiration. To mask her self-consciousness, she busied herself pouring out the lemonade into plastic cups and handed him one.

"Your name — Ardith — I've always wondered about it. It's so unusual. Is it a family name?"

"It's a combination of my parents' names, Arthur and Judith, Ardith, see? My mother told me they wanted something that suggested I was part of both of them, of their love for each other."

"Beautiful!" he commented, impressed by the idea.

A companionable silence followed as they helped themselves to the food and sipped their lemonade. The woods were very still around them, and yet the rush of water over stones in the brook below them, the flutter of bird wings high in the trees above, and the hum of insects in the wildflowers provided a symphony of nature.

"This is pure poetry," Gavin said finally.

"Do you still read and collect poetry, Ardith?"

Ardith looked at him, her eyes wide.

"You remember?" She had forgotten she had told the young Gavin one of her best-kept secrets. Most men would have thought her silly and sentimental.

"I probably remember everything you told me about yourself," Gavin said solemnly. Then he began very quietly to recite. " 'Come live with me and be my love, and we will all the pleasures prove of golden sands and crystal brooks —' " He halted. Looking at Ardith intently, he asked, "Will you, Ardith? 'Come live with me and be my love'?"

She returned his look and question. "Do you mean — ?"

"What I said."

"I don't know, Gavin. You promised not to pressure me. It's too soon for either of us to make any kind of commitment, to know if —"

"Know if I love you? I knew that the first time I saw you again. It was all mixed up then with anger and shock and — but it was there, as strong as I remembered it. It's there now. I love you and I want you to share my life."

"Your life is so different now," Ardith replied. "I don't see how I'd fit into such a glamorous —"

"Glamorous!" Gavin broke in, sitting bolt upright. "You think my life is *glamorous?* There's nothing glamorous about getting on and off jet planes, being in one strange city and hotel after another. It all begins to look and feel the same, packing and unpacking, being alone. That's what it means most of all — being alone."

"Alone?" She scoffed gently. "With all your adoring fans vying for a few minutes of your time, an autograph? I saw what happened after the concert at Everett, Gavin."

He looked at her skeptically. "That doesn't always happen, believe me. That's a press agent's dream. Mostly people hardly notice. Oh, if I have to attend a sponsor's reception after a performance, a few people might lionize me. But mostly my life on the concert tour is boring, except for those terrible moments before a concert. I actually used to be sick before one. Now, I've trained myself to handle that — but the nerves, the feeling that I might fail, forget the piece, stumble, play the wrong notes —" He flexed his fingers at the recollection of his fears.

"Ardith," he declared vehemently, "if

you were with me, it would make all the difference in the world. I'm tired of being alone. But there was never anyone I wanted to be with other than you. Finding you again is like a miracle. Now I know what my life has been missing all these years. Please say yes to me."

Ardith was speechless. His outburst had been so dramatic, so volatile, she did not know how to reply to it. She prayed silently for the right words.

"Oh, Gavin, I can't. Not yet. There's still so much we need to discuss, to know about each other. We need to be together now to learn to know each other as the people we've become. We can't decide anything as important as marriage on the basis of a few days —" She hesitated, then continued. "I'm trying to be honest with you, Gavin. I don't think I could share your life as it is now."

"I may not go on with this kind of life much longer," he said seriously. "I have maybe two more years of concert bookings, not all of them confirmed. And now that I'm well established, there could be more recordings, longer rests between engagements. Less of this gypsy life.

"I've even thought of teaching. At the music department the other day I enjoyed all those eager young people. I felt a real excitement about helping them. I think I really might like a college post. You'd like that, too, wouldn't you?"

Ardith smiled. "You'd probably find it very dull in time."

He frowned, then said archly, "I think life is only dull to dull people."

She laughed lightly. He leaned over and put his hand on her cheek.

"I love your laugh," he said tenderly. "And your eyes and your nose and your mouth," he continued, kissing each feature. "As a matter of fact, I love everything about you. And I can feel you still love me, too. Of course, there's a lot we'll both have to adjust to, but I can make changes if I can just know that you'll be with me. I can't lose you again."

"Please, Gavin, you said you wouldn't pressure me."

"Darling, I don't mean to. I just need to know that you will consider it seriously, that you will give us a chance."

"Yes, I can promise that. It's important to me, too."

He jumped to his feet, reached down for her hands, and pulled her up and into his arms. Slowly he lowered his face to her lifted one and kissed her, a kiss that Ardith had no will or wish to resist. Finally, with deep sweetness, it ended.

They stood looking into each other's eyes for a long time before Ardith reluctantly broke the spell.

"We'd better start back now. It will be getting dark soon —"

"I love you," Gavin said.

"I know," she answered with a shy smile. Their arms around each other's waist, they started slowly back through the shadowy woods in silence. When they emerged into the meadow edging on the orchard, the day seemed to darken quickly.

"We should hurry," Ardith said, quickening her step, but before they reached the steps to the front porch, Gavin held her back. His cheek was cool from the brisk wind as he pressed it close to hers, but his mouth was warm as he kissed her once more.

"Just so you won't forget all that I said today." He pulled her close. "Promise? You'll give me some hope, some reason to believe our love means as much to you as it does to me? To find out if we can begin again?"

"Yes, Gavin, I promise!"

His arms went around her, holding her close.

Just then, Ruff came around the house with a welcoming bark and came up to them, his head nudging against them. They both laughed and moved apart.

"I need to let Gran know we're back, Gavin," Ardith said softly.

He leaned down to pat Ruff and said, "Okay, I'll be in in a minute."

Ardith looked at the pair affectionately, then ran up the porch steps and into the house. She went into the kitchen to return the empty picnic hamper and found her grandmother in the pantry arranging some shaggy white and gold dahlias in a vase.

"Enjoy your picnic?" Mrs. Fielding asked.

"Oh, yes, it was great!"

Her grandmother took a long-stemmed dahlia and clipped it slantwise. "Charles came by, brought a nice brace of quail, so naturally I asked him to dinner."

"Tonight?" gasped Ardith.

"Why, yes, tonight. Anything wrong with that?" Mrs. Fielding asked in mild surprise.

"No, I guess not. I just thought with Gavin here —"

"It might upset Charles? He knows we have a guest. I told him," Mrs. Fielding said calmly.

"Of course, he doesn't know about Gavin —"

"If he had known, I might not have asked him. He's always been in love with you, you know."

Ardith said nothing. She waited a minute, then asked, "Is there anything I can do to help?"

"No, thank you, darling, not a thing. I have everything under control in the kitchen. After all, Charles is practically family, so there's no fuss."

"Well, then, I'll go shower and change," Ardith said and gave her grandmother's shoulders a hug.

She and Charlie Mercer had practically grown up together. His family's farm bordered the Fieldings', and they had been playmates as children. Later when he was at military school and she at the nearby girls' boarding school, he had come over to visit on weekends, handsome in his cadet uniform. He had been her staunch friend in the aftermath of her marriage. But she could never feel love, the kind that is fire and ecstasy, for Charlie. Ardith knew Charlie loved her, but she had carefully avoided providing an opportunity for him to declare it.

When she was at Sunnyfields they saw

each other but almost always in the company of her grandmother or other friends.

Something warned Ardith, however, that tonight she would have to make sure nothing betrayed her feelings for Gavin while Charlie was here.

She hurried through her shower and dressing, wanting to be on hand in case Charlie should arrive early. Gavin, in his present elated mood, might let something slip about the two of them. If there were anything to tell Charlie, she wanted to be the one to tell him.

She opened her closet and studied its contents, trying to decide what to wear. At Sunnyfields her grandmother wanted her to wear a dress for dinner, especially when there was company. After a minute's indecision, she chose a dusty rose wool, its simple lines softened by crocheted edging at the neck and wrists. As she brushed her hair, she considered letting it hang loose the way Gavin loved it, then thought better of it and swiftly drew it back and up, securing it into her usual style with silver-tipped combs. If she and Gavin were dining alone, it might be different. But they weren't. And with a final look in the mirror of the pine dressing table, Ardith started downstairs.

When she walked into the living room, Gavin was sitting on the sofa and turning the pages of her grandmother's photograph album. At her entrance he looked up and smiled. "I'm finding out all about you. How you looked at ten, as the sweet girl graduate, and — where were you going looking like this?" he asked, pointing to a picture of Ardith in an off-the-shoulder white bouffant dress and long white kid gloves. She held an old-fashioned bouquet in a lace paper frill.

"Oh, *that!* It was taken at my 'coming-out' party, the cotillion. It's a Melrose tradition," she explained. "Grandmother and my mother insisted I go. Most of us — the girls whose families have lived here forever — felt it was a bit — much. I mean, to introduce young women to society in this day and age seems a little outdated to say the least. But we went along with it."

Gavin gazed at her steadily. "And you're afraid of moving into *my* kind of life? *I'm* the one who should feel uncomfortable in your world. After all, I'm just a poor farm boy from Kansas. I'd still be there, milking cows, feeding chickens, driving a tractor, except for something inexplicable —" He held up both hands and moved his fingers as if on a keyboard.

"Background and birthplace are things you have no control over. It's the rest of your life, what you do with it, that counts," Ardith responded quietly.

"Worlds apart to begin with, now here, together." Gavin closed the photo album and spoke with careful casualness.

"By the way, there are no pictures in here of you as a bride."

"I took them out, long ago," she answered tightly.

"Some day I want to hear about your marriage. When you're ready to tell me, of course," Gavin said evenly.

At that precise moment Mrs. Fielding entered the room and there was no time for a rejoinder. "Well, Mr. Parrish," she said, "what do you think of Sunnyfields now that you've had the opportunity to see more of it?"

"It's as close to heaven as I can imagine on this earth," he smiled. "I only wish I had some place as peaceful and permanent to come back to after one of my tours." Spontaneously Mrs. Fielding glanced at Ardith to see her reaction to Gavin's remark, but before either of them could comment, the front doorbell chimed. Charlie Mercer had arrived.

No two men could have been more different than Charlie Mercer and Gavin Parrish. Physically they were direct opposites.

Gavin had dark, rather continental looks, a trim, taut body, quick movements, dramatic gestures, and cosmopolitan manners while Charlie was lanky, sandy-haired, rugged, and outdoorsy.

Charlie was Melrose County personified — old family, old money, and absolute confidence in background and breeding, which showed in his well-worn good tweeds, Brooks Brothers shirt laundered thin, and knit tie. He made Gavin, in his butter-yellow suede sport coat, precisely creased slacks, and Italian loafers, look too urbane, too expensively tailored.

Almost immediately the two men seemed to know instinctively they were rivals. Throughout dinner a subtle yet tangible undercurrent could be felt. Even their conversation was competitive. For all of Charlie's frequent protests that he was only a country lawyer, he was a clever one. Tonight he was exhibiting some of his skills. Without seeming to, he led the talk to topics Gavin obviously was ignorant of or had little interest in, and he did it so smoothly it was imperceptible to everyone but Ardith. The fact that Charlie was "at home" at Sunnyfields and Gavin was a guest, a stranger, an outsider became more and more apparent as dinner progressed. When Mrs. Fielding suggested they have their coffee in the living room, Charlie rose at once, picked up his plate, and followed her into the kitchen to help carry in the coffee service. Gavin got up also and stood awkwardly for a moment as if not sure what to do.

Without realizing it, Mrs. Fielding compounded his uncomfortable feelings by saying quickly, "Oh, no, Mr. Parrish, do go in the living room with Ardith. Charles will help me."

Only Ardith noticed the flush on Gavin's face as he offered her his arm and they left the dining room together.

Later as they all were gathered in front of the fire having their coffee, Charlie, elaborately casual, asked Gavin, "How long do you plan to be in Melrose, Mr. Parrish?"

Ardith stiffened, noting Charlie had been careful to say Melrose, not Sunnyfields.

When Gavin answered that he had to leave Sunday because his tour was starting the next Tuesday, Charlie drawled indifferently, "Strange kind of a life, I imagine."

"Perhaps, but it gives me the opportunity to meet all sorts of people, to see places, and experience things I couldn't otherwise. Of course, it has its drawbacks —"

"I would think so," Charlie shrugged. "Travel should be a pleasure, not a job."

Gavin flushed again, and he was flexing his fingers, as he did so often when tension rose. But Ardith saw with admiration that he was not going to allow himself to be drawn into an argument with Charlie.

"Do you have much time to yourself on tour to visit some of the museums and art galleries?" Mrs. Fielding asked.

"Not as much as I'd like. My time is usually taken up with practice. As soon as I get to the city where my concert is scheduled, I have to go to the hall to test the instrument and the acoustics —"

"What a shame! Imagine being in Madrid and not being able to go to the Prado or in Paris and not go to the Louvre," said Mrs. Fielding with real sympathy.

"Did I tell you, Miss Charlotte," Charlie interjected, "that I got to the limited exhibit of the pre-Raphaelite painters at the Tate when I was in London?"

A quick glance at Gavin's surprised reaction told Ardith that Charlie's knowledge was a total shock to him. Now Charlie was waxing eloquent about Burne-Jones and the other painters whose works he had seen at the exhibit. He had summarily dismissed Gavin and seemed to find it important that Ardith be impressed by his trip to London.

Even though she understood Charlie's motives in a way, Ardith was annoyed by his tactics. She knew Charlie was a Harvard graduate and in the top ten of his law class at the University of Virginia, but he didn't need to flaunt it.

Every once in a while, Ardith caught Gavin looking at her with tender intimacy, as if he knew his position with her was assured. So all poor Charlie's efforts were in vain.

When Charlie finally left, Mrs. Fielding politely stifled a yawn and excused herself for the evening. Pleading sleepiness herself, Ardith told Gavin she also must go to bed.

"If you don't mind, I'd like to read in the library for a while," he said.

"Why no, Gavin, of course I don't mind. Gavin — when I visit Sunnyfields, Grandmother and I go to an early church service Sunday mornings. You're welcome to come with us if you'd like."

"Of course I'll come," he said without

hesitation. Then he grinned. "I grew up going to church twice a week and twice on Sundays."

He came over to her and put both hands on her shoulders, and looking down into her eyes, he smiled. "We've still got a lot to learn about each other, haven't we, darling?"

He leaned down and kissed her, a long, lingering, infinitely tender kiss.

The sweet, familiar longing she always felt in Gavin's arms swept through her with strange, mysterious fire. She had never been more aware of her own yearning to give in to it, to abandon herself to the exquisite pleasure of belonging to Gavin at long last.

Gavin's voice in her ear spoke urgently of love. Over and over he whispered her name.

But no! Not again, never, would she act on impulse, no matter how strong the desire, how urgent the need. She had not come this far to make another mistake.

After a long while, she pushed gently away.

"Good night Gavin," she said breathlessly, and she hurried out of the room, across the hall, and up the stairs.

As she ran up the stairway, she could almost feel his eyes following her, his heart calling her back, but she rushed down the hall and into her room.

If they were right for each other, they would know it. Ardith was convinced God would show her. Until he did, she would wait.

Chapter Six

The Melrose Community Church was much as it had been in colonial times. Simple in design, its white and blue painted interior created an atmosphere of dignity and peace.

The raised front pews had little doors on the outside. And each door had a small brass plaque engraved with a family's name.

Rigid under the almost tangible scrutiny of the regular church members, Ardith stood while Mrs. Fielding unlatched the door of the Fielding pew, stepped up, and entered.

Seated between her grandmother and Gavin, Ardith was intensely conscious of both. Glancing at her grandmother's aristocratic profile under the brim of her gray, satin-trimmed hat, Ardith was reminded of an exquisite cameo with fine, fragile features and a strong yet compassionate mouth. Dressed with understated elegance in a bouclé suit and a strand of pearls, her composure was as constant as the familiar fragrance of Parma violets she always wore.

Ardith was even more conscious of Gavin's presence on her left. He was looking straight ahead, occasionally lifting his eyes to study the arched rafters and the numbers on the hymnal board, his expression unreadable.

What was he really thinking? Feeling? Did he feel strange or out-of-place in this little country church, with her beside him, after all these years and all the places he had been?

How different from her own life in the same span of time! Her brief, unhappy marriage had been a travesty of real love. Since then, she had been preoccupied with building a wall to keep herself safe.

If she and Gavin should marry, would it be possible for him to take the vows to love, cherish, and honor her? Could she dare to believe that Gavin would make the lifelong commitment a truly Christian marriage demands?

Almost as if aware of her thoughts, Gavin turned his head, and their eyes met and held. Their gaze lingered until broken by a general movement around them as the congregation stood to the opening music from the old wheezing organ.

As they came out of church, Ardith

caught a glimpse of Charlie, but her grand-mother had stopped to talk to friends and was introducing Gavin, so Ardith was un-able to wave to Charlie or speak. She would have to drive back to Everett in the morning, and she at least wanted to say good-bye. Something about the stiff set of his shoulders made her feel he was un-happy. She tried to catch his eye but his head was averted, and he got into his car and drove off without looking her way.

Back at Sunnyfields Ardith cooked a big, country breakfast, just as she had when she was a girl with Cora in the kitchen coaching. She put the sausage and scram-bled eggs into an ornate silver chafing dish and set it on the sideboard. After they had served themselves, they sat at the round table in the sunny kitchen.

"Will you do the honors, dear?" her grandmother asked Ardith indicating the silver Sheffield coffee urn in front of her.

Just as Ardith began to fill their cups with the dark, richly pungent coffee, Gavin addressed her grandmother. "Mrs. Fielding, I want to marry your granddaughter."

The silver pot felt suddenly heavy in Ardith's trembling hand, and she nearly dropped it. Her grandmother, however, did not indicate any surprise. She responded to Gavin in a calm voice.

"And have you asked her?" The blunt question was softened by her southern accent.

"I'm hoping to enlist your help in persuading her." Gavin glanced over at Ardith, a glint of amusement in his eyes. "I think I'm having some problems convincing her that it's right."

"I never give advice — at least not on the subject of love or marriage," Mrs. Fielding said smoothly, putting down her cup. "There's too great a margin for error. Besides, you both are mature people who certainly don't need my help on such a decision."

"Gavin!" Ardith remonstrated. "It's too soon to drag Grandmother into it. You promised to give me time."

Gavin made a great display of putting out his wrist and looking at his watch. Shaking his head, he said playfully, "Time's running out for me. We'll have to leave for the airport soon. I just thought we could get your grandmother's blessing."

Mrs. Fielding looked from one to the other. "You do have my blessing, both of you. I bless you by praying that you will be given the wisdom to know what is right for both your lives." She paused, smiling.

"What more can I say?"

An hour later they had loaded the car and Gavin turned to Ardith's grandmother to thank her earnestly for her hospitality. "And believe me, Mrs. Fielding, I love your granddaughter very much, and I think I can make her happy."

Mrs. Fielding smiled in reply. "Happiness comes from within a person, Gavin. No one can make another person happy. I wish you the best for yourself and Ardith."

On the way to the airport they stopped for coffee at a charming restaurant, the Stagecoach Inn. The dining room had a colonial atmosphere and appropriately costumed waiters and waitresses. After they had ordered, Gavin said, "Your grandmother is a very wise woman. And beautiful, like her granddaughter." He smiled and reached across the table to take Ardith's hand.

"You know, I was serious when I told you I want to cut down drastically on my concert tours. I'm really dreading this tour facing me now. Finding you again makes me realize how empty my life has been without you, how much I want and need you in my life."

Ardith said nothing, and Gavin went on. "Please, darling, let your answer be soon and let it be yes!" He leaned forward eagerly. "There's so much I want us to do together. We should go to the museums and the theater. And we can! I can reschedule my life to do more recordings, fewer concerts.

"My next tour ends in San Francisco the last week in December. Meet me there. We'll have almost a week together before my next concert. There'll be no pressure for commitment, I promise. I just want us to have time, unhurried time, to spend together, to sort things out, to get to know each other better. This weekend was a wonderful beginning, but we need more. What about it, darling? San Francisco, the week after Christmas?"

As she drove back alone to Sunnyfields, Ardith felt devastatingly lonely. She had watched Gavin run up the steel steps to the plane, turn at the top to wave, then disappear inside. That was when the strange, new loneliness had begun.

All along the road to Sunnyfields the woods on either side seemed to loom darkly. When she had reached the crest of the hill where her grandmother's acreage began, the sky was gray with clouds that deepened her depression.

She parked her car in the driveway and

hurried up the porch steps, hoping her grandmother would be waiting for her. But the living room was empty, and again she felt that strange loneliness.

Outside, the light was disappearing fast. Ardith shivered and went over to the windows to pull the curtains shut and she saw the delicate branches of her grandmother's young maple trees bending in the rising wind. Ardith felt as if she, too, were in the path of a storm. Gavin's reappearance was like the swift onset of a wild gale sweeping into her life.

"Why don't you put on some light, dear? It's very gloomy in here." Her grandmother's voice behind her startled Ardith, and she whirled around to see her moving about turning on lamps. A comforting glow leapt into the room. Mrs. Fielding struck one of the long fireplace matches and put it to the fire already laid. Soon the snap of kindling sounded, and the logs began to leap into flame.

She turned to her granddaughter, her head to one side, and studied her with concern.

"Well? Did Gavin get his answer?"

"He got an answer. I'm not sure it's the one he wanted or if it's the right one."

Her grandmother continued to look at

her speculatively, then sat down in the wing chair and took out her needlepoint. "And what exactly does that mean?" she asked quietly.

"He'll be in San Francisco at the end of his tour in December. He wants me to come out there then, spend the holidays with him and then make a decision."

"And will you?"

"I've told him I would." Ardith paused for a second, then explained, as much to herself as to her grandmother. "He feels we'll have a chance then to see how it would be to be together without pressure, without the conflict of our separate lives. Our being together these few short days has been too chaotic for us to evaluate our feelings rationally."

"In other words, it's too sudden. Is that what you mean?"

Ardith nodded, smiling slightly. "Right, exactly."

A silence fell and both women stared into the firelight, busy with their own private thoughts until Mrs. Fielding spoke again. "Of course, my concern is about his lifestyle. I can't imagine anything much more different from what you're used to."

Her grandmother frowned and took several stitches before she continued. "You're beautiful, intelligent, charming. Why on earth would you want to complicate your life by marrying someone temperamental, tempestuous, difficult? There are other men in the world besides Gavin Parrish."

"You mean, like Charlie?"

"Like Charles, of course. He's been in love with you for years. I think if he dared to think it possible, he would propose in a minute."

Ardith shook her head, smiling almost sadly. "Oh, Grandmother, I love Charlie — but I could never be *in* love with him. And if I've learned anything, I've learned how wrong it is to marry someone you don't love."

"Many marriages — good ones — are based on respect, esteem, mutual faith, background —"

"No, Grandmother. Not for me."

Silent, her grandmother went on with her needlepoint, and Ardith stared into the fire.

Finally Ardith spoke, almost to herself. "Maybe I'm tired of being alone. I've been alone a long time. But then, so have you, Grandmother. Aren't you ever frightened of being alone?"

"There are worse things than being alone. Being lonely is one of them." Mrs.

Fielding peered over her demi-glasses at Ardith. "Then you will go out to California in December?"

"Yes — in December," Ardith said slowly. Even to herself her voice sounded somewhat uncertain.

There was frost on the ground the morning Ardith left Sunnyfields and started back to Everett. The long, lazy days of Indian summer were now gone. The halcyon few days with Gavin were also over, and Ardith began a period of stark, cold consideration about the future.

She had promised him she would meet him in San Francisco the week after Christmas. But now, without his dynamic presence, Ardith wondered if she should have made that promise.

The next few weeks at Everett were full. November and early December were always particularly busy with special events on campus. Two different guests in the cultural program stayed at Bower House, and each proved especially challenging for Ardith. The first, a pretentious Englishman lecturing on the Far East, required a strict diet of special herbs and exotic fruit. The next was the soprano for whom Gavin had substituted, a prima donna with a

Mediterranean temperament.

Ardith was used to handling most situations, but with the departure of Elena Romani, she breathed a sigh of relief.

It was now Monday of the third week in November, and Ardith was involved in planning a gala Thanksgiving party for the international students, their guests, and others who lived too far to travel home for the five-day holiday.

She walked across the campus toward Bower House. She had just stopped at the post office to pick up her mail in which she found a short, hastily scribbled note from Gavin from Houston, Texas, demanding the date he could expect her in San Francisco. His notes were more often than not followed by long-distance calls. He never gave her enough time to answer one before another arrived or a call came.

Ardith was deep in thought, so preoccupied by the thought of Gavin and the trip to California that her name was called twice before she turned to see Annalee Bridges, one of her favorite students, running to catch up with her.

"Mrs. Winslow!" she called breathlessly. "Mrs. Winslow, may I talk to you for a minute? Do you have time?"

"Why, certainly," Ardith answered,

waiting until Annalee was beside her.

Annalee tucked her long, wheat-blond hair behind her ears with a nervous gesture and panted, "I need some advice, Mrs. Winslow. Before the Thanksgiving vacation."

"Well, I hope I'm the one to give it to you," Ardith said doubtfully as they started toward Bower House.

"If you can't, I don't know who can! You're — well — so *together*, Mrs. Winslow."

"Well, I can try!" Ardith smiled. She noticed that the pretty young face looked troubled. "Would you like to come over to my apartment for a cup of tea?"

Annalee gave a quick glance at her wrist watch, then shook her head. "I have a class in fifteen minutes. Could we find a place to talk somewhere on campus? The quadrangle, maybe?"

The quadrangle was a sunny enclosed place between the science building and the gymnasium, with built-in recessed benches.

"Sure, why don't we go over there now?" Ardith suggested.

Once seated, Annalee seemed to have a hard time getting to the point. Finally she blurted out, "It's my boyfriend, Mrs.

Winslow! He's at Cragmont, a senior."
Cragmont was a men's college near
Everett. "He's not living in the dorms any
more. He's got an apartment." Annalee
paused hesitantly. "And he wants me to
move in with him next semester." She finished in a breathless rush, her round face
flushing.

"What should I do, Mrs. Winslow? He
says if I love him I'll move in with him and
I do love him, but, well, I don't — really
think it's right. Lots of people are doing it,
I know. And it may sound square or
prudish or — Ken says reactionary — but
somehow I just feel it may spoil things for
us —" Annalee shrugged. "But I do love
Ken, Mrs. Winslow. A whole lot!"

"How old are you, Annalee?"

"Nineteen."

Ardith drew her breath in sharply. Older
than she had been when she fell madly in
love with Gavin. If living together had ever
come up, what would she have done? She
had to ask herself that honestly before she
could answer Annalee. She closed her eyes
for a silent prayer. *Dear God, help me to be
gentle with this child! I feel so inadequate.
Lord, give me the right words.*

Ardith laid her hand affectionately on
Annalee's arm. She spoke very softly, "You

are a very sweet, very special person, Annalee. I'm sure Ken loves you, but does he love you enough to understand you're uncomfortable about what he's suggesting? I know you're a Christian, but I don't know if Ken shares our belief that belonging to each other physically is very precious and should wait until marriage.

"Anything less than total commitment might destroy the very thing Ken loves most about you." She paused. "If he really loves you, I don't think he would want you to do anything that would hurt your own feelings about yourself."

Annalee's brown eyes grew bright with tears. "Oh, Mrs. Winslow, I know you're right. I just got so confused. When I'm with him, it's so hard to — well, you know." She wiped at her eyes with the backs of her hands like a little girl.

Ardith's heart wrenched painfully. She reached out and brushed back a strand of blond hair that had fallen over Annalee's downcast face. "I don't know if you'd want to, Annalee, but I go to a Bible study at Dr. and Mrs. Hawkins' house every Wednesday evening. Maybe you'd like to go with me tomorrow night. It's a good mix of ages, personalities, and Dr. Hawkins leads the discussion. Right now, we're studying

Paul's teachings on letting the Holy Spirit guide us in our decisions."

Annalee bit her lip thoughtfully as if trying to make up her mind. Then in a rush she said, "I have a test Thursday, and I should study on Wednesday — but I'll do it tonight instead! Yes! I'd like to go, Mrs. Winslow."

"Good. I'll pick you up at your dorm at about seven-fifteen, all right?"

"Okay, it's a deal!" Annalee jumped up and glanced at her watch. "I've got to dash or I'll be late for class. Thanks, Mrs. Winslow. You're the greatest!"

Ardith watched the slim, young figure run across the quadrangle and sprint up the steps of the science building, her long, blond hair flying behind her.

The conversation with Annalee brought her own confusion over Gavin sharply into focus. She thought of her own reaction to Gavin, that powerful attraction surging through her when he took her in his arms. It was as strong now as it was their first night on the moonlit deck ten years before. Ardith felt a little shiver. Who was she to advise Annalee?

Her phone was ringing when she got back to Bower House, and she hurried to unlock her apartment door.

"Ardith!" The deep, resonant voice sent an electric tremor through her, making her fingertips tingle and her wrists weak. It played on her spine as if it were a reverberating musical string.

"Gavin," she sighed.

"I'm in Detroit and it's snowing and I miss you terribly. My plane was delayed four hours and I just got in. I feel awful. My head's aching and I think I'm getting a sore throat and I have this dreadful ache inside of me — just to see you, to hold you! I don't have time to go to the concert hall to rehearse, and I know I'm going to botch tonight's performance."

Ardith cradled the receiver on her shoulder and stripped off her gloves, smiling. She had received this kind of call from Gavin in Pittsburgh, Cleveland, and Baltimore. She was beginning to recognize his pre-concert nerves.

"Oh, Gavin, I'm sorry. Have you taken some aspirin? Call room service for some tea and lemon and honey. I'm sure you'll feel better and play splendidly as usual." She tried to make her voice soothing and reassuring.

But he would not be soothed nor reassured.

"I don't think I can get through the rest

of the tour," he said gruffly. "It's too long to be without you."

"It will be only a few weeks," she remonstrated gently.

"Too blasted long. I keep thinking we should be together. Being apart doesn't make sense. I wish you were here with me right now."

"I do, too, Gavin," she said impulsively.

"Then fly out to me here. Make the rest of the tour with me."

"Oh, Gavin, you know I can't —"

"Why not?" he demanded stubbornly.

"I can't just drop everything here. This is a particularly busy time. With the holidays coming, lots of programs are planned for the college. A guest lecturer is arriving at Bower House tomorrow."

Her rush of words was received with silence on the other end of the line.

"Well, I'd better go."

"Gavin! Don't forget the tea —"

"Right, I won't."

And then he was gone.

For a few seconds Ardith stood holding the phone. A dozen conflicting emotions rushed through her: sadness for him alone in that faraway hotel feeling ill and depressed, melancholy for her own sharp memory of his arms, and longing to be held by him again.

An involuntary shudder swept over her. Everything she felt for Gavin was contradictory and intense. She had reacted to him physically with all the passion of her first love, but now that he was gone she was racked with doubts. She still did not really know the man Gavin had become.

Since he had held her and kissed her good-bye after their weekend at Sunnyfields, Ardith had regretted her promise to meet him in San Francisco. In retrospect it seemed a rash thing to do. Several times she had sat down to write him, but she had never been able to finish the letters. She had always torn them up and tossed them away as his memory overcame her with such force and reality she felt as if he were standing beside her. Then, the old loneliness had come unbidden, almost suffocating her.

She knew that she could not have an answer to the doubts in her heart unless she went out to California to spend those days with Gavin.

Wednesday evening Annalee was waiting on the steps of her dorm when Ardith pulled up in front. She came running and got into the car.

"All set for the test tomorrow?" Ardith asked.

"Well —" Annalee dragged the word out doubtfully. "Not as much as I should be. The truth is, Mrs. Winslow, after our talk the other day, I was so excited, so sure of myself, that I called Ken. I guess I should have planned more how I was going to say what I wanted to say — well, I just blurted it out. About how I don't think it's a good idea for me to move in with him and — he got just furious! It ended up in a huge fight and he hung up." Annalee sighed heavily.

"So I stayed up talking to Jill and crying most of the night and didn't get any studying done. I almost called you earlier to tell you I couldn't go to the Bible study. But, then, I thought, why not?" She sounded forlorn and hopeless.

"I'm sorry, Annalee, about the quarrel with Ken. But I'm glad you decided to come tonight anyway. The Bible study might help," Ardith told her.

Mrs. Hawkins met them at the door and welcomed them, ushering them into the living room where people were already sitting and chatting everywhere — on the floor, in the comfortable chintz-flowered chairs, and on the circular sofa. Many nodded and smiled at the newcomers as they came into the room. Some greeted Ardith by name.

Annalee saw someone she knew and found a seat beside her on the floor, while a young, bearded man stood up and offered Ardith his chair.

Dr. Hawkins, a pleasant, soft-spoken, graying man in his forties, casually dressed in a sweater and cord pants, quietly opened the meeting.

"For those of you who are new here with us this evening, welcome!" He smiled around the gathering. "We always begin with a prayer to quiet ourselves and to enter the presence of our Lord."

The room grew very still. In a low voice he began. "Heavenly Father, we come this evening with all our burdens, all our wandering thoughts, all the things in our lives you already know about, and we ask you to come in your own gentle way and make your presence known to us as we study your Word."

After the opening prayer there was a period of silence for private prayer. Ardith was engrossed in her own petitions when she heard Dr. Hawkins's voice begin the study. "Last Wednesday, we were in First Corinthians, chapter six. If someone will begin reading at verse twelve, we'll continue around the room, everyone taking a verse through verse twenty."

After the reading, Dr. Hawkins asked a few questions to initiate a lively discussion of the Scriptures. But in no time at all it seemed the hour was up.

"For those of you who are with us for the first time tonight, we invite you to join us next week. And keep in mind that the library is still open for anyone who wants to get some studying in." He paused. "We'll close with a prayer and then anyone who would like to stay for coffee and more talk is welcome."

This time everyone stood and clasped hands in a circle for the closing prayer.

There was a resounding "amen" from the group, followed by strong handshakes all around the circle as the group broke up.

Back in the car Annalee was very quiet and Ardith was not quite sure why. They drove back to the campus and pulled up in front of Annalee's dorm. But she made no move to get out of the car.

"What is it?" Ardith asked gently.

Annalee shook her head, but in the light shining from the dashboard of the car and from the lamppost outside the building, Ardith saw tears glistening on Annalee's cheeks.

"Oh, honey! Tell me," she said, reaching over to clasp Annalee's hand clenched tightly in her lap.

Annalee shook her head and struggled to speak. "It was just — just so beautiful!" Her voice wavered. "I mean that part about our bodies' being the temple of the Holy Spirit and that we don't belong to ourselves but we were bought at a price." She went on, a sob in her voice, "And it's so true! The other night Ken kept saying, 'It's our business what we do. We're not hurting anyone.' But we would be! I see that now."

Ardith said nothing. There was no more she could add to the lesson Annalee had learned through God's Word.

Annalee pushed open the car door.

"Thank you, Mrs. Winslow, for taking me tonight. I really appreciate it!"

Back at Bower House, Ardith donned her robe and slippers and put the tea kettle on to boil. She would make herself some instant cocoa and unwind. But her mind, just like Annalee's, had been stimulated by the Bible study. It was so relevant to what was going on in her own life. She had not pinpointed it until that moment — or perhaps she had simply not wanted to face it. Gavin, all enthusiasm, all ardent excitement about moving forward with their lives had shrugged away her argument about how much they had changed since their first blinding rush of love. He seemed to think they could pick up their lives again just where they had been broken off and live happily ever after. But that was an ending for fairy tales.

The tea kettle whistled, and Ardith stirred in the cocoa mix, set her mug on the kitchen counter to cool a little, and went in search of her Bible.

Holding it to her, she closed her eyes and prayed a prayer from Exodus 33:13 and 15. She had prayed the prayer often before but never with more earnest pleading.

"If I have found grace in your sight, show me now your way —" She modified the rest to make it more personal. "If your presence does not go with me, do not lead me from here."

If she should not go to San Francisco, Ardith wanted to know. She was asking for some sure sign. She did not want to fling herself headlong into a mistake.

She replaced her Bible on her bedside table and went back out to the kitchen. Sipping the cocoa slowly — so reminiscent of the childhood bedtime cocoa and animal crackers — she smiled to herself. Was she unconsciously seeking the comforting security of bygone days?

The more she thought about that the more she felt she needed to reach out, to read her Bible, to search for the possibilities it offered. She had been so proud of the safe life she had made for herself at Everett. Could God want her to risk that life, want her to find enough security in him to cross the country and find out if she could share Gavin's life?

She was a grown woman, twenty-eight. She had handled her circumstances well enough for the last few years. But now she would turn to her Bible. She would let God speak to her, as she wished she had all along. As a result, she felt a calm in her very center.

Ardith quickly got out her Bible and read far into the night. Again and again she was drawn back to Exodus 33.

She decided to memorize some of the verses. Then whenever she felt that stirring of indecision, that twinge of panic, she could pray the words of Scripture.

Even now they seemed to give her peace. She closed the Bible, glad that she had followed her leading to study it afresh. It was just what she had needed to do.

Chapter Seven

Gavin sent Ardith airline tickets early in December, and the trip to San Francisco seemed real at last.

As she drew them out of the long envelope and looked at them, she murmured, "Well, here it is, 'for better or for worse.'" Then she realized with a start what words she had quoted.

Since she knew the next few weeks at Everett would be full of preholiday activities, Ardith drove into town on Saturday to complete her gift shopping. She found herself instead trying on clothes in an expensive shop. Lured by an attractive outfit displayed in the window, Ardith went in to find something suitable for her California trip. She would need some special things for going out with Gavin, who was surely used to elegantly dressed women.

It had been a long time since she had shopped with the idea of pleasing a man, but as she began to choose things Gavin might like, Ardith realized she was enjoying herself. Trying on various outfits was fun. The saleswoman was delighted and kept bringing things into the dressing room. She saw at once that Ardith was discriminating, but she didn't expect her to be extravagant. As Ardith's selections began to pile up in the dressing room, the woman looked at her customer speculatively. Then she asked, "Is it for a special occasion?"

Ardith was trying on an apricot ultrasuede suit. "Very special."

The woman eyed Ardith cautiously. "A honeymoon?"

Ardith turned around, a secret smile lifting the corners of her mouth. "Perhaps," she parried. She glanced once more at the price tag, and deliberately dismissing the exorbitant cost, she said, "I'll take it."

On the way back to Everett, the back seat of her car stacked with boxes, Ardith felt excitedly lighthearted. She was satisfied with her purchases, and the thought of actually wearing them for Gavin sent her thoughts spinning happily ahead.

As she entered her apartment, she was smiling to herself. She dumped her packages and automatically went to check her telephone answering machine for messages. Then she checked her desk calendar for appointments. What she saw made her laugh aloud.

The famous quotation at the top of the page for this Saturday was, "Beware of all enterprises that require new clothes." *It's a good thing Henry Thoreau can't see me now,* she thought.

The last week before Everett closed for the Christmas holidays, Ardith had a full schedule of events to be held at Bower House.

The house was beautifully decorated with a six-foot tree in the foyer and garlands interwoven with scarlet satin ribbon on the front door and on all the front windows. Vases of fresh holly and red and white poinsettia plants enlivened the rooms with color. Red candles accented the shining brass and crystal prism holders on the mantel, buffet, and dining table. Visitors flowed through the house almost every day for some social event. The International Students' tea, the senior banquet, the Choral Society's concert reception, and the Drama Club's Christmas party were all hosted at Bower House.

Tomorrow everyone would be leaving for the holidays and a candlelight service was being held in the campus chapel. Then the faculty and guests were invited to a party at Bower House. After Ardith had dressed in one of the new outfits purchased for her trip, a cranberry raw silk two-piece, she checked to make sure that everything was ready for the party and then started for the chapel.

An atmosphere of hushed expectancy permeated the candle-lit interior. As if from afar — the distant hills of Judea, perhaps — rose the sound of high, sweet young voices singing "Hark, the Herald Angels Sing" and coming closer and closer. The young women dressed in red and white chapel capes filed into the raftered chapel and took their places in the choir stalls at the front. Listening to the ringing clarity of the glorious words, Ardith was almost overcome with a sense of the past.

"A thrill of hope, the weary world rejoices . . ."

The carols brought memories of past Christmases, both happy and unhappy, as well as the promise of the unknown ones to come. This could be her last Christmas concert at Everett.

As the last chorus of "Joy to the World!" resounded in the high-ceilinged chapel, everyone joined in. The glee club came down from the choir and walked up and down the aisles shaking hands as they sang "We

Wish You a Merry Christmas." It was a beautiful and joyous finale, and Ardith felt a happy excitement as she hurried back to Bower House to greet the first guests at the party.

The next afternoon, driving out through the now-deserted campus, Ardith thought about Annalee. She had seen the young woman only once since the Bible study early in December. She had not wanted to seem to be pressuring her, but she'd prayed that Annalee would continue to attend the Bible studies. She hadn't, but then final exams were held before the holidays, and Annalee was probably swamped with studies. At least, that's what Ardith hoped the reason was. She hoped Annalee was not avoiding her.

She had seen her once in the cafeteria, and their encounter had been brief, the conversation hurried. All Annalee had said was that she and Ken were spending Christmas with their families but planned to go skiing together afterwards.

Annalee had not said if they were going with a group or alone, and of course Ardith had not asked.

She said a prayer for her young friend, knowing how great her temptations were, how hard her decision. After all, Ardith herself still did not know what Gavin expected of her when she got to San Francisco.

Now that the surrounding trees were bare, Sunnyfields stood out plainly in the winter sunshine. As she turned into the driveway, Ardith saw a wreath, bright with holly berries, on the front door.

Inside, a twelve-foot cedar, awaiting its traditional Christmas Eve trimming, was already standing in the semicircle at the foot of the curving staircase, its tip reaching up higher than the second-floor balustrade. It filled the house with its spicy scent.

Preparations were well under way for her grandmother's Christmas Eve supper party. Every year for as long as Ardith could remember, friends had been invited to help trim the tree and share a bountiful buffet. The Christmases Ardith had spent in Florida, she had been almost sick with longing to be celebrating the holidays at Sunnyfields. If she married Gavin and had to be in some faraway place at this time of year, would she still be homesick?

The days flew by as Ardith helped her grandmother wrap presents, make cranberry-orange relish, polish silver, and wash the delicate crystal goblets and the special china, Lenox "Holiday" pattern with handpainted holly trim.

As they worked, they talked about family, friends, the small events in each of their lives since Ardith had been there at Thanksgiving. Her grandmother did not ask her about Gavin until Ardith brought up the subject herself.

"So you think being together in San Francisco will give you the answer you're looking for?" Mrs. Fielding asked.

"I hope it will."

"But won't it be difficult to picture an ordinary, everyday sort of life together in a glittering, glamorous place like San Francisco?"

"I don't think life with Gavin would ever be ordinary or everyday, no matter what the environment." Ardith smiled ruefully.

"That's just what I mean, Ardith." Her grandmother put down the piece of silver she was rubbing and spoke seriously. "I'm worried about the whole idea of your going out there, as if somehow you'll get a magical solution to a situation fraught with complex issues and complications."

Ardith reached over and patted her grandmother's arm comfortingly. "I know you hoped I'd eventually settle down with — someone like Charlie. But I can't just let Gavin go out of my life again without seeing if it can work."

"You're right, of course, and I'm wrong to try to influence you." Mrs. Fielding took up the serving fork again and the chamois cloth and began polishing vigorously. She smiled, then added, "I hope you're praying about this."

"I am, Gran. I am," Ardith assured her gently.

Early Christmas Eve afternoon a light, powdery snow began to fall, and before Ardith and Mrs. Fielding had left for the first evening service at Melrose Community Church the ground was blanketed in white.

As the organ sounded, Ardith took her place beside her grandmother in their pew and picked up the small, worn red hymnal from its rack. She turned to the number designated on the bulletin and sang "Good Christian Men, Rejoice." The voices of the congregation filled the small church with loud joy.

After the warmth of the church, the night air seemed especially cold and clear. The sky was a dark canopy studded with bright stars. The cheery sound of "Merry Christmas" rang out with peals of laughter as neighbors mingled in the frosty evening before heading home.

As Ardith and Mrs. Fielding started toward the station wagon, Charlie Mercer came running over to them.

"Miss Charlotte, Ardith, wait!" he called. "A white Christmas this year after all! And guess what, I got out the old sleigh as soon as it started snowing. Just had a feeling —" he laughed heartily, rubbing his gloved hands together. They turned in the direction he pointed, and sure enough there stood an old-fashioned red sleigh right out of a Currier and Ives print. "Could I talk you two ladies into a sleigh ride over to Sunnyfields?"

"Oh, thanks, Charles, not me," Mrs. Fielding declined. "I think I'm a little too old for that. Besides I've got guests coming, so I'd better get home and see to things. Thanks just the same. Cora has been helping me, but I'm sure she'd like to get home to her own family for supper. Her children and grandchildren usually gather at her house before the midnight service." Mrs. Fielding glanced over at Ardith. "Why don't you go, Ardith? Sleigh riding on a starry night is for young people!"

Charlie turned eagerly to Ardith. "What do you say, Ardith?"

"Well, if you're sure you don't need me

at home, Grandmother," she answered with a slight note of hesitation.

"No, honey, Cora probably doesn't even need *me!* You go along with Charles."

"If you're sure, then, Miss Charlotte. Come on, Ardith. Let's go!" Charlie smiled and took Ardith's hand.

They hurried over the snowy ground, breaking the crust that was already forming on the top. The two horses hitched to the sleigh were stamping their feet, blowing through their nostrils, and shaking their bell-trimmed harnesses. Charlie helped Ardith into the seat and tucked a robe around her knees.

"Will you be warm enough?" he asked.

"Oh, yes!" Ardith assured him, pulling her woolly, white knit hat down over her ears and turning up the wide collar of her red coat.

Charlie hopped in on the other side and picked up the reins.

"All set?" he asked.

"All set!" she said. "This is going to be great. I can't even remember when I've ridden in a sleigh —"

"The winter before you went to Europe," Charlie told her.

The winter before I met Gavin, Ardith remembered.

With the sharp jingle of sleigh bells echoing through the clear crisp air, they started off. Ardith felt pure elation as they skimmed over the fields and onto the less-traveled back roads. The air was so cold her eyes stung and it almost hurt to breathe. The wind whistled past her as the runners cut into the snow behind the two trotting horses.

"How're you doing?" shouted Charlie, looking over at her.

"Wonderful!" Ardith shouted back, laughing. When they reached Sunnyfields, it looked like a Christmas card, the roof white with snow and the lighted windows shining bright rectangles onto the snow-covered yard.

"Whoa!" shouted Charlie, pulling up on the reins. The horses came to a reluctant halt. "I guess I'd better take them around to the barn and look after them. I'll let you out here."

She pushed aside the robe and started to get out of the sleigh, but Charlie took her arm.

"When are you coming home for good, Ardith?" he asked in a low voice.

"Home?"

"Yes, to Sunnyfields, to Melrose. You belong here, you know."

At that moment the front door opened, and Ardith was saved from having to answer his question by her grandmother's call.

"Telephone for you, Ardith. Long distance."

Without a backward look Ardith sprang out of the sleigh and ran up the steps and into the house. She felt sure it would be Gavin.

It was. He was in Los Angeles and on his way to a party his manager had arranged for him to attend after his concert.

"Some wealthy matron in Beverly Hills," he growled. "A patron of the arts." He mimicked an affected voice. "She supposedly can do a lot to promote me. Ardith, I wish you were here. Or I were there! That we were together anywhere."

"Gavin, I'll be there on the twenty-eighth," she said patiently, smiling at his eagerness and feeling her heart leap at the longing in his voice.

"That seems an eternity! Why wait until then? Why not come sooner?"

"I can't change my reservations this late —"

"How can I wait three more days?" he groaned.

"You'll have to — and so will I," Ardith said softly.

"I love you!" Gavin said intensely.

"I know."

"Tell me you love me, too, darling," he commanded.

Ardith's heart pounded. She had not yet made that declaration. Could she now?

"We'll be together soon, Gavin. I'll tell you then."

"I'm pressuring?"

"A little, yes."

"All right. I'll try to be patient."

When Ardith had hung up and gone to join the party in the living room, Charlie gave her an odd look. Her grandmother raised her eyebrows slightly, came to her side, and whispered, "Those stars in your eyes give you away!"

Ardith just smiled. Catching a glimpse of herself in the mirror, she knew that she was radiant with happiness.

The evening passed pleasantly. Trimming the tree was fun, and the huge buffet was sumptuous. Everyone enjoyed the traditional turkey, cornbread dressing, sweet potato soufflé, hot rolls, creamed onions, and snap beans. Dessert offered a choice of pecan pie or ambrosia, a southern compote of fresh oranges, bananas, and coconut. Of course, everyone took a piece of the Sunnyfields specialty, a dark, rich fruitcake.

Charlie was one of the last guests to leave, and Ardith walked him to the door. There he hesitated significantly and looked at her with serious, troubled eyes.

"Ardith, I'd planned to ask you to marry me when you came home this time. We have so much — we've grown up together. I think I've always thought that some day —" He paused awkwardly and gave a short laugh. "Lawyers are supposed to be good with words — eloquent, even! You should hear me in a court room, but now — anyway, I've decided to risk asking you even though I wondered about — that guy, the pianist who was here a couple of months ago."

Charlie stopped suddenly as though he had seen something in Ardith's face that gave him his answer.

"That's it, isn't it? You're in love with him. So, there's no use, is there? I don't have a chance."

Impulsively Ardith reached out both hands toward him. "Oh, Charlie, I'm sorry."

Charlie nodded grimly. "I should have known." He put his hand on the doorknob, then leaned forward and kissed her cheek. "I guess I'll have to accept it. Good night, Ardith. Merry Christmas!" He went quickly out into the night.

Feeling both touched and a little saddened by Charlie's sincerity, Ardith went back into the dining room where her grandmother was clearing up the serving dishes.

"It was a nice party, wasn't it?" Mrs. Fielding smiled. "And such a beautiful service at church. I believe it was the loveliest ever."

Ardith began gathering the scattered Christmas plates and carrying them out to the kitchen. As they worked in accustomed rhythm, the only sounds were the occasional tinkle of crystal and china. The dining room still glowed with candles and the lights from the Christmas tree.

It was Ardith who broke the silence. "Charlie asked me to marry him tonight."

After a pause, Mrs. Fielding said, "And — ?"

"Of course, I said I couldn't."

Silence fell once more. Mrs. Fielding placidly worked on. Then she spoke quietly. "All this will be yours some day, you know. There's no one else. I sold another twenty acres to Charles last year, the acreage that borders on the north pastureland. He's doing a magnificent job with that land, Ardith, planting soybeans and alfalfa and shipping the excess to third-world countries. He tithes most of it. He's a fine man. It would be a good thing if you and he —"

"Grandmother!"

Mrs. Fielding shook her head. "I'm sorry, my dear. Just wishful thinking, I guess."

"I know Charlie is a fine, wonderful person but —"

"You don't love him —"

"Not that way!"

Her grandmother's hand touched her hair, and she leaned against the older woman's shoulder.

"I know you wish things were different, Grandmother," she sighed.

But Mrs. Fielding said quickly. "All I want is for you to be happy, Ardith. I just pray that whatever you decide, those stars in your eyes tonight will always be there."

The last dish dried and put away, grandmother and granddaughter sat down before the multicolored flames of the yule log in the fireplace. As Christmas Eve became Christmas morning, Mrs. Fielding worked on her needlepoint, and Ardith gazed silently into the dancing flames.

Chapter Eight

Ardith had to change planes in Chicago for the balance of her trip to the West Coast. But when she checked in at the desk she was told her flight to San Francisco would be delayed because of bad weather. Momentary panic followed the pang of disappointment.

Her first thought was Gavin's reaction. He had sounded impatient enough last night when she talked to him. Now there would be still further delay.

She started to the row of pay phones, then halted. How could she reach Gavin to tell him about the situation? He would have already left for the airport. She could imagine him characteristically pacing and flexing his hands. Surely, he would know by now that her plane was getting in late, and he would be frustrated, irritated at the delay.

She walked back across the lobby past the cocktail lounge and gift shop and stopped at the newsstand with its pyramids of paperbacks. She studied titles and jacket blurbs, searching through mysteries, romances, westerns and sci-fis, until she found C. S. Lewis's *Miracles*, one of his books she had not yet read. Dr. Hawkins had recommended the author to her, and he had become one of her favorites as he awed her with his ability to be both humorous and profound.

She bought the book, which she took to the coffee shop. Reading Lewis would be a pleasant and profitable way to spend the hours before she arrived in San Francisco.

Eventually her flight was called. Ardith boarded, found her assigned window seat, and settled in. Her heart accelerated. She was now setting out on the last leg of her trip. Gavin would be waiting for her at her journey's end.

Needles of sleet tattooed the window as the plane taxied to the end of the runway, passing other aircraft. Ardith's pulse pounded with the roar of the giant engines preparing for takeoff. Then came the thrusting sensation of speed as the jet lifted, and they were airborne.

The flight attendants started rattling their trolleys of drinks down the aisle, and Ardith adjusted her seat to a more comfortable position. There was no longer any chance of not going to San Francisco, no turning back. She was on her way to whatever lay ahead.

The busy weeks at Everett before the holidays plus the stress of the delayed flight had made Ardith more tired than she had realized, and she slipped into sleep. She only vaguely recalled refusing the drink offer and lunch. The next thing she heard was the attendant's voice on the intercom, "We are making our final approach into San Francisco —"

Blinking her eyes, Ardith sat up and leaned forward to look out the small window. She saw a curve of blue bay below. The sun was shining, its reflection on the plane's wing tip blindingly bright. How strange to leave Chicago in the beginning of a blizzard and arrive a few hours later in sunny California. A light happiness bubbled up inside her. She could not help humming under her breath the familiar tune about San Francisco opening its Golden Gate.

Her heart thumped madly, and her throat was dry with excitement as the huge jetliner touched down.

Here she was at last! And now what?

She took her mirror out of her purse, touched her nose lightly with powder, and smoothed on fresh lip gloss. Did she look all right? How would she look to Gavin?

She had last-minute second thoughts

about her outfit. Was it right for California? The royal blue knit under the belted gray suede coat had seemed right when she chose them. Worn with a black velvet tam, a black shoulder bag, and high-heeled boots, Ardith hoped she had achieved a look stylish enough for sophisticated San Francisco.

Now the covered walkway was being fitted into the plane's door. People crowded into the aisle, anxious to deplane. With a deep intake of breath, Ardith slipped her bag onto her shoulder, picked up her neat carryon, and started toward the door.

Ardith moved into the terminal that was teeming with activity. Immediately she saw Gavin standing right at the edge of the roped-off area, towering above the crowd. He waved both arms. In one hand he was clasping a small bouquet.

Suddenly she felt as giddy as a school-girl. The next moment he was rushing forward and swinging her up in his arms, lifting her off her feet.

"You're here! You're really here! I can hardly believe it!" He looked down at her with shining eyes, then frowned. "Are you worn out by all the delay?"

Dazed with happiness, Ardith shook her

head. "I slept on the plane," she told him.

He tucked her arm into his, pressing it tightly against his side. "We'll go claim your baggage. Then I've a car waiting, and we'll go right to the hotel."

He had hardly finished speaking when they were halted by several voices calling his name. "Mr. Parrish! Can you give us a minute, sir?" Gavin squeezed Ardith's hand and whispered, "Oh, *no!* Reporters! But don't worry. I'll handle it."

Just then a flashbulb nearly blinded her. Gavin's arm went around her protectively, and she heard him groan under his breath.

But he said jovially, "Okay, fellows, please! My friend would prefer not to be photographed. But I'll be happy to pose for you alone." He shrugged smilingly as if to share with them a laughable idiosyncrasy on Ardith's part.

Giving her a few curious looks, the reporters reluctantly moved with Gavin a little apart from her. He carried on a bantering conversation with them as they took shot after shot. He answered some questions and fielded others, and within a few minutes the reporters thanked him and left.

A small crowd had gathered outside the circle of reporters and now clustered about him thrusting boarding passes and other scraps of paper at Gavin, asking for his autograph.

Finally, Gavin held up his hands in smiling protest.

"Ladies, gentlemen, you're going to miss your flights!" he backed away to rejoin Ardith and then propelled her swiftly and smoothly through the lobby.

"I'm sorry, darling," Gavin scowled. "I didn't think about being recognized but I suppose all those new posters about the concert tomorrow night have made me pretty identifiable. But how could they have known I'd be here?" Then his lips tightened. "Renay! She never misses a chance for some publicity!"

"Renay?" Ardith echoed, puzzled.

"Renay Easton, my manager and agent," he replied shortly, his hand tensing on her arm.

At the luggage carousel they got her suitcase, then hurried outside. There a steady stream of cars was depositing and picking up people in a cacophony of shouting voices, roaring motors, and public address announcements. Out of the line of cars a long gray limousine swerved to the curb, and a uniformed driver leapt out, ran around, and opened the car door for them, tipping his hat as he did so.

Once they were inside the luxurious limousine, Ardith leaned back against the velvety maroon upholstery, and Gavin slid his arm around her shoulders. As the car pulled smoothly out into the traffic, Gavin sighed with relief.

"That's over. Now, let me look at you. I can hardly believe you're here, in my arms!" He turned her face up toward him, and his eyes seemed to embrace her.

Slowly he drew her closer and kissed her, a kiss that stunned her with its intensity. Deeply stirred, she realized that his kiss was erasing all the anxiety, doubt, and uncertainties about the journey. Simple joy to be with him welled up within her.

On either side of them, traffic was moving at a dizzying pace, but inside the car, time seemed to stand still.

"*Now* I know it's real," Gavin breathed as the kiss ended. "What a day I've had. Up at dawn. Couldn't sleep. Then couldn't eat. Couldn't wait at my hotel, so I came out two hours before your arrival time. Then they told me about the delay. It's been awful.

"This morning the first thing I thought was 'Ardith will be here in just a few hours!' " He hugged her again and touched her cheek. "I love you! Did I tell you that?"

They kissed, and it was a long time before either spoke. Finally Ardith said, "You mentioned a concert tomorrow. I thought your tour was over."

"It was. It is," he answered, "but Renay arranged it. It's a benefit for some eminently worthy cause. She told me it was worth a million dollars in publicity. You know agents lie awake at night dreaming of ways to get good press. Well, this was practically handed to us."

He shrugged. "So! It will mean only a few hours of our time. Then we're free. Oh, darling, there are so many things for us to do together. I'm so glad you're here, so glad you came!"

They were in the city now and soon drove up the long hill into the sweeping curve of the driveway in front of the elegant Nob Hill Hotel.

After the doorman greeted them and handed Ardith's suitcase to the bell captain, Gavin escorted her through the palatial lobby. At the desk he was greeted deferentially by one of the clerks and handed a sheaf of messages. Then Gavin introduced Ardith as his guest and waited until she was registered and given keys to her room.

As they moved toward the elevators, he raised an eyebrow and spoke in a low tone. "You're on a different floor from my suite, so everything is being conducted properly." There was a tinge of suggestive teasing in his words, and Ardith felt herself blush. She had not wanted to admit to herself her concern that Gavin might not have fully understood her conditions.

In the elevator he looked at her tenderly but did not speak further. Ardith was aware that a few of the other passengers glanced in Gavin's direction then back again, as though they recognized him.

The doors slid open for them and Gavin's hand on her elbow gently guided her down the long, thickly carpeted corridor and into a T-shaped wing at the end. Then he inserted his key-card into a door and opened it into a mirrored foyer. He held the door for her to enter first.

When Ardith hesitated, Gavin explained. "This is my suite. There's a powder room where you can freshen up if you wish. You can go down to your room later, but I wanted you all to myself first. We haven't had a minute alone since you got off the plane."

But they were not to have even that minute. As they stepped inside, a woman's voice called out from another room. "I'm in here, Gavin, and I have some marvelous news!"

Ardith glanced quickly at Gavin, puzzled. There was something about him that should have warned her. He was suddenly all tension; a muscle in his jaw tightened. But there was no time for an explanation because a moment later a tall blond woman appeared in the archway leading down to the sunken living room of the suite.

She was wearing a black pantsuit with a diagonal band of vivid red slashed across the jacket, and Ardith's first impression was of dramatic beauty. A second, more discerning look belied the illusion of artful make-up. The hair was surely platinumed, worn in a severe style to emphasize her enormous dark eyes fringed with lashes so long and curving, Ardith was certain they were false. But the overall effect was glamour personified.

"Hello there. You must be — Ardith," the woman said in a low throaty voice with a slightly patronizing overtone.

Then quickly her eyes dismissed Ardith and moved to Gavin where they focused. She flashed a brilliant smile. "Congratulations, darling! We did it! The contracts with Templeton are being drawn up now. Melbourne, Hong Kong, Tokyo, here we come! We're going to celebrate the best deal I've arranged for you yet!"

Gavin seemed to struggle with both anger at the unexpected intrusion into a private moment and excitement at the news of the contracts.

Smiling confidently, the woman had already started back into the living room. "You'll be so pleased with the concessions I got them to make," she said over her shoulder. "First cabin all the way, deluxe accommodations everywhere, choice of instruments — everything you asked for and more!"

Finally Gavin was in control of his mixed feelings. "Bravo, Renay! If anyone could pull it off, you could." He took Ardith's arm and smiled at her. "Come along, darling. I'll introduce you properly to Wonder Woman — my agent and manager, Renay Easton."

Accompanying Gavin into the living room, Ardith's first sweeping impression was of space and a width of windows around a creamy rug, pale green walls, rounded plush chairs, a modular sofa, and a grand piano. *This must be one of the VIP suites,* she thought.

On the free-form, glass-topped coffee table was a silver, ice-filled bucket in which a tall-necked bottle was chilling. Melba toast rounds surrounded a bowl of shiny, dark caviar and three long-stemmed glasses were on a silver tray.

"Do you want to do the honors, or shall I, Gavin?" Renay asked, making a graceful gesture toward the bottle.

Gavin was helping Ardith off with her coat. "I'll do it. But wait — Ardith doesn't drink champagne. Do we have anything else?"

Renay looked surprised and flicked an astonished glance toward Ardith. "A martini, then? Or — ?"

"No, I meant Ardith doesn't drink."

"Not at *all?*" Renay seemed shocked. "Not even for this special celebration?" Her voice was now edged with sarcasm.

Gavin ignored her tone. "We have Perrier, don't we?"

"Oh, please, don't bother," Ardith ventured, embarrassed by the fuss.

"I *could* call the bar and have them send up a Shirley Temple —" Renay said with a little laugh.

"Renay, we must have something. Would a cola do, darling?" he asked Ardith.

Her face flushed, Ardith nodded. "Fine."

With a few long strides, Gavin crossed the room toward a small kitchen area.

Left alone with Renay, Ardith felt extremely uncomfortable. Even though Renay was occupied inserting a cigarette into a long ivory holder, Ardith felt the woman's eyes moving over her, taking her measure. It was the kind of survey a woman sometimes made of — a rival.

Soon Gavin was back with an iced soft drink in a glass. "Here you go, darling." He smiled at Ardith reassuringly.

Then he turned to Renay. "All set now. Let's drink to my tour and its success!"

The champagne was uncorked and poured. Renay and Gavin toasted each other happily, while Ardith sipped her drink and tried to recover from the intense awkwardness of the situation.

Putting down his glass and ignoring it completely, Gavin began to ask questions about details of the contract and upcoming tour. Directing all her conversation to Gavin, Renay acted as if Ardith weren't even in the room.

After a while, Gavin put his arm around Ardith's shoulder. "Sorry darling, this must be boring you. That's enough shop talk and business for today, Renay. We can settle up anything else later. Remember,

I'm on holiday — starting now!" He spoke good-naturedly but definitely, the tension in his hand signaling his impatience.

"Well, I can take a hint!" Renay said, with elaborate emphasis. She stood up and took a final sip of champagne before she set the glass down delicately with finger-tips sporting long, polished nails. "I'll leave you two to your — your long-awaited — reunion." She smiled, but icily.

"I'll be on my way. And, Gavin, I'll be in touch first thing in the morning." She paused and then with a raised eyebrow and feigned innocence added, "You will be here in *your* suite, won't you?"

Hot color rushed into Ardith's face at Renay's innuendo.

Gavin got to his feet and spoke curtly. "I'll see you out, Renay."

Ardith's fingers tightened on the glass she was holding. Why was Renay being deliberately rude?

As their discussion lengthened in the hall, Ardith walked over to the wall of window on the other side of the room and looked out.

It was beginning to get dark, and lights were coming on all over the city, turning it into a fairyland of sparkling color. San Francisco, with all its glamour, magic, and glitz was waiting for her to explore it. She was here at last, and she had no idea what lay ahead in the next few days.

Just then she felt Gavin's arms slip around her waist and his cheek bend to hers. She heard his voice whisper tenderly in her ear. "And now, darling, our time begins!"

Chapter Nine

Since Ardith had never been with Gavin before a concert, she had no idea what to expect the next afternoon when she took the
elevator up to his suite. She had not seen
him all day because he had spent the time
preparing for his performance, first prac-
ticing, then resting.

"Once this benefit concert is over, we'll
have all the time in the world to ourselves,"
he had promised the night before when he
kissed her good night at the door of her
suite.

Ardith smiled, remembering their evening together, her first in San Francisco.
They had dined in one of the smaller
dining rooms of the hotel, a beautiful room
of flowers, white latticed walls, and Victorian decor, where they were seated at a se-
cluded corner table by the maître d' and
served by an attentive waiter. No one hov-
ered as she and Gavin lingered over their
meal. Obviously the staff was accustomed
to celebrity guests, being neither overawed
by them nor unduly fawning.

Dinner was uniquely Californian cuisine

— breast of chicken, rice pilaf with mushrooms, and a salad of avocados, pineapple, and papaya. Gavin sipped a light wine while Ardith had a sparkling Calistoga water with a slice of lime. With their coffee came fresh pears and Brie.

Their conversation had been the one of lovers long separated, filled with broken sentences, interruptions, and long silences when they simply gazed into each other's eyes. There was so much to say to each other, yet neither seemed to be able to find the words.

"I wish this concert hadn't been arranged," Gavin said with a shrug, "— but it has. I'm through regretting things I have no power to control — like the past!" he said significantly.

He leaned forward across the table, and his hand touched the one she instinctively extended. "The future is what's important! *Our* future, Ardith. I hope you feel the same way."

Ardith looked into the eyes riveted on her so questioningly. How could she answer? She still felt disoriented, transported so swiftly from everything familiar into Gavin's world of limousines, VIP treatment, exclusive restaurants, expensive hotel suites —

161

The room Gavin had reserved for her was really a suite with its dressing room and bath off the bedroom. A huge brass bed covered with lacy pillows was at one end of the bedroom and graceful Victorian velvet armchairs and a loveseat furnished the alcove at the other end. A bouquet of fresh white and red gladioli was centered on the coffee table in front of the white marble fireplace.

Staying at this hotel was like being a pampered guest at a luxurious private home. There were all sorts of unexpected amenities, such as the fluffy terry cloth robe in the bathroom and the delightful surprise of finding the bed turned back for the night, a single rose and a gold-foil-wrapped chocolate left on the scented pillow.

Gavin had grown accustomed to this atmosphere of glamour, excitement, and exotic accommodations, which dazzled Ardith and frightened her a little. It was too heady an environment for making a decision that would change her life dramatically and forever.

Her fingers touched his across the table. "After the concert, we'll have time to talk —"

The waiter, coming to refill Gavin's

coffee cup, interrupted further discussion, and Ardith began to feel tired from her long day of excitement, travel, and airport delays.

When they had finished their coffee, she said regretfully, "Suddenly, I'm exhausted, Gavin. I'm afraid I'll have to call it a night."

"That's all right, darling. I like to get a good night's sleep before a concert anyway. After that —" He smiled. "There's so much in San Francisco I want to do and see! And it will be so much fun to do it together — with you!"

She had slept late, breakfasted in the hotel's coffee shop, then gone on a little exploring trip of her own, leaving Gavin undisturbed until later in the day.

The city in all its holiday glitter enchanted her. She stopped to watch a troupe of mimes at Union Square, listened to a band of street musicians play jazz, gazed at the fabulous window displays at Macy's and Neiman-Marcus. She selected strawberry crepes at a restaurant that offered a dozen varieties and returned to the hotel to rest, bathe, and dress for the concert.

Now the elevator doors slid open at Gavin's floor, and Ardith, stepping out, stopped to check herself in one of the mirrors opposite before starting down the carpeted corridor to his suite.

Her outfit, one of the special buys for this trip, was the right choice for the occasion. It was subtly elegant, and the saleswoman who had assisted her had declared she looked stunning in it. Its vivid turquoise was becoming to her eye and hair coloring, and the fitted jacket and slim skirt emphasized her model-slim figure. She hoped Gavin would like her in it, too.

But when she arrived at his suite, she found Gavin too nervous and distracted to be aware of anyone else, even though he greeted her with affectionate warmth.

When he led her into the living room, Ardith was dismayed to see Renay seated on one end of the modular cinnamon velour sofa. One leg tucked under her and the other swinging indolently, a loose high-heeled pump dangling from her toes, Renay was sipping a glass of wine.

The two women exchanged stilted greetings, and Ardith sat down at the opposite end of the couch. She tried to be at ease while the other woman observed her with an amused expression.

Renay was certainly striking, Ardith had to admit, dressing effectively to dramatize her moonlight-blond hair and dark eyes. Today she was wearing a lipstick-red wool dress cut superbly to compliment her curves and her long, spectacular legs sheathed in dark hose. Her chunky jet necklace and matching earrings enhanced the sophisticated look.

Ardith's attention, however, did not linger long on Renay. It was Gavin who disturbed her by his complete preoccupation.

He paced back and forth across the long room. He clenched his hands, then unclenched them. He walked over to the piano, lifted the lid, stood there for a minute, then trailed his fingers along the keys, running up and down a scale. Then he whirled around to retrace his steps back and forth, flexing his fingers constantly.

Finally, uncomfortably nervous, Ardith stood up. "Perhaps I'd better wait in my own room or, better still, take a taxi to the concert hall." She made a movement toward the door.

But Gavin was at her side immediately. He put both hands on her shoulders. "No, of course not, darling. I want you here. I need you here."

So, reluctantly, Ardith had remained, feeling awkward and in the way as Gavin

continued his self-involved pacing and
Renay sat idly turning the pages of a
fashion magazine.

At last it was nearly time to leave for the
concert hall, and Gavin went to change,
leaving the women alone in the strangely
quiet room. The silence rang with deaf-
ening undercurrents, undercurrents Ardith
did not fully understand but of which she
was agonizingly conscious.

She glanced at Renay who was looking at
her speculatively. As their eyes met, Renay
drawled, "Well, this is how it is before
every concert! Think you could take it?
Over and over, ad infinitum?"

Ardith was unable to think of an answer,
and a long, tense moment stretched like a
high, tightly wired rope ready to snap until
it was broken by Gavin's appearance.
Handsome in his tails, stiff white-front
shirt, white bow tie, he replaced their tension with his own.

The three of them went down the elevator together, not talking, wrapped in
Gavin's contagious anticipatory tension.
Ardith was silent, afraid that something
she might say or do would inadvertently
upset Gavin's concentration.

Then they were walking through the carpeted splendor of the lobby out into the

crisp, early evening air to the waiting limousine, which whisked them along the foggy city streets.

Ardith got out in front of the main entrance of the concert hall. Gavin kissed her lightly on the cheek before she was assisted from the deep-cushioned interior of the limousine by the uniformed chauffeur. She looked back, but Gavin's head was already turned toward Renay who was saying something. Then the long, shiny car pulled away from the curb, and she was alone.

Ardith took a deep breath, her nervousness gradually easing. As she went up the steps of the concert building, she found herself asking the question Renay had put to her earlier: *Think you could take it — over and over?*

She was ushered to her seat and she settled in, opening her program. All around her the murmur of conversation floated, as the audience filed down the carpeted aisles, took their places, rustled their programs, greeted one another. Anticipation filled the auditorium.

Then as if by a secret signal, the noise diminished, the magenta velvet curtains began to rise, and an expectant hush fell. A moment later Gavin walked out onto the stage, and like a waterfall, applause broke through the audience, crashing noisily all around and resounding in Ardith's ears.

They like him, she thought. *They know he's good.* Her heart was pounding as Gavin bowed and moved toward the gleaming black concert grand piano.

The applause died down, again as if from a hidden signal. Ardith held her breath unconsciously, watching Gavin sit down, adjust the seat, flex his hands, pull down the cuffs of both sleeves, then rest his hands on his knees for a moment, tilting his head slightly back as if in meditation. Then finally, he placed his hands on the keys and the first notes rippled out, and Ardith, along with the rest of the audience, was caught up in the mesmerizing magic of Gavin's virtuoso performance. This time Ardith thrilled to "Clair de Lune" and the "Apassionata" as joyously as she had ten years ago.

Later a crush of people backstage crowded the narrow hallway toward Gavin's dressing room. Ardith was turning back to wait for him in the lobby, but just then Gavin, towering over the group clustered in front of the doorway, saw her. Moving through them with his massive shoulders, he caught her by the arm and literally elbowed their way back into the relative safety of his dressing room.

The buzz of greetings, congratulations, kudos, and praise was loud and confusing. Finally, the combined efforts of Renay and the stage manager maneuvered most of the people out and away. They closed the dressing room door firmly on a few persistent diehards.

Gavin collapsed in the nearest chair, stretching his long legs out in front of him. Letting his arms drop on either side and his shoulders sag, he let out a prolonged sigh. "Whew! That's over! I lived through it!"

He looked utterly drained.

Renay went to him and began to massage his neck. Gavin groaned ecstatically.

"Good! That's good," he murmured, closing his eyes wearily.

Looking over his head at Ardith, something strange and curiously elusive flickered in the dark brown depths of Renay's eyes.

"Let's get out of here," moaned Gavin.

"I've already called the driver," Renay replied soothingly.

Inside the limousine, Gavin slumped against the plush gray upholstery and leaned his head back against the cushioned head rest. His eyes were glazed with fatigue. He reached for Ardith's hand and said apologetically, "I'm not much good after one of these, darling. I'll make it up to you tomorrow."

"Headache?" Renay asked.

"The beginning of a beastly one, I'm afraid," Gavin responded, rubbing one hand over his forehead and eyes.

When they got to the hotel, Renay took charge at once.

"He'll need to take a pill and sleep. He's had it for tonight. The only thing that helps is complete rest," she told Ardith, dismissing her.

In the elevator, his topcoat draped over his evening clothes, Gavin leaned against the wall, his face drawn and haggard. Renay pushed the button for Ardith's floor without consulting her. When the doors opened, all she said was, "Here's your floor."

"Good night, Gavin. I do hope you feel better —" began Ardith uncertainly.

He took her hand, raised it to his lips, and kissed it. "Sorry, darling, I'm washed out. I'll be fine in the morning. I'll call you, first thing."

As the elevator doors closed quietly behind her, Ardith felt rejected, abandoned. Shouldn't she be the one to care for Gavin now? She felt displaced by Renay.

She walked slowly down the corridor to her room and let herself in. She undressed and put her things away mechanically, her thoughts completely taken up by the events of the evening. A montage of scenes and impressions crowded in on her, too many and too confusing to define.

She had had a miniglimpse into Gavin's life, and she felt impressed, frightened, and intimidated — a dozen emotions jockeyed for attention. But one feeling dominated the others.

Ardith knew she loved Gavin with all her heart.

Whether she could love him with all her strength and soul she did not know. And whether that love could overcome the obvious hurdle of Renay's possessiveness also remained to be seen.

The one thing that was clear to Ardith about Gavin's life was Renay Easton's attachment to Gavin and her hostility toward Ardith. The woman had unmistakably flung down the gauntlet of challenge.

Chapter Ten

"Why are you smiling?" Gavin asked Ardith, looking at her from behind dark glasses.

"I'm thinking how incredible it is to be sitting outside like this in December!" she laughed.

They were at the rooftop restaurant of Ghiradelli Square the afternoon following the concert.

"You're in California!" Gavin flung out his hands and lifted his shoulders as though that explained everything.

"Somehow I feel like Alice in Wonderland and I've just stepped through the looking glass," she said, looking about with pleasure, the sun warm on her back. Against the cloudless blue sky half a dozen Chinese kites of various sizes, shapes, and colors danced in a frantic ballet from where they were being flown on the marina below.

Gavin leaned forward across the glass-topped table and said in a low voice, "You look absolutely beautiful!"

"Beauty's in the eye of the beholder, Gavin!" She shook her head slightly, but still smiled. She felt relaxed and happy. All the tension of the concert was gone.

"Well, then, I'm beholding beauty," he replied, looking at her tenderly. She was wearing a tangerine silk shirt, a bouclé-knit cardigan in a light coffee color, and matching pants. The sun, slanting in under the striped umbrella that shaded their salads and iced tea, sprinkled her dark hair with lively golden lights.

True to his promise and evidently completely recovered from his exhaustion of the night before, Gavin had called Ardith before ten that morning and had shown up at her room as she was finishing the coffee she had ordered from room service. He'd looked refreshed and energetic in an open-necked jersey, gray slacks, and a yellow windbreaker.

They had spent the morning walking and window shopping, stopping occasionally to make a quick tour of a gallery. They had then gone to the old brick Ghiradelli chocolate factory, now a multistoried beehive of boutiques, fascinating shops, and intriguing stores of all kinds.

When they had ended up on the top floor to have lunch outside, it was nearly empty except for a few latecomers like themselves. At the entrance they'd noticed a poster announcing the benefit concert, and Gavin slipped on dark glasses.

"Not that anyone would recognize me," he shrugged. The poster was a very modern arty one, a two-tone photo image in which Gavin's dark hair was tousled as was becoming to a creative artist. His dark eyes dramatically moody, he appeared to be the classic sensitive musician.

Ardith wondered where the real man behind the image was. Was he something his press agent had created, or was Gavin, after all, the man he said he was, the man who loved her, wanted her to become part of his life? She still did not know the answer.

Basking in the balminess of the sunny afternoon, Ardith was half-daydreaming when she became aware of Gavin's eyes thoughtfully gazing at her.

She felt sweet surprise at his unabashed feelings for her. Under the intensity of his gaze, she lowered her eyes in sudden confusion, her long dark lashes making twin shadowy crescents on her flushed cheeks.

"I absolutely adore you," Gavin said huskily.

It was a moment of happiness, pure and unflawed. Ardith slowly raised her eyes to look at him. He reached across the table, his fingers encircling her wrist, and a flutter of sensation swirled through her.

"Have you thought any more about us, Ardith? Doesn't being together again seem the most natural, the right thing — ?"

"Oh Gavin —" She started to tell him some of what she had thought about them and life together the night before when she had lain awake in the dark, when sleep had eluded her.

But she never had a chance. Almost at once she heard her name.

"Ardith?"

Startled, Ardith automatically twisted around.

"Ardith Winslow! I thought that was you, but I wasn't sure!" Ardith stared at the speaker in disbelief. A well-dressed woman with a champagne beige, bouffant hairdo came toward her around the tables. A middle-aged, balding man was close on her heels. The Prescotts! Friends of her mother and Curtis's from Key Mirador, Florida! Elaine Prescott was talking a mile a minute as she neared their table.

"I told George the minute I saw you, 'Why that looks like Ardith Winslow,' and he said, 'Why, it couldn't be, what would Ardith Winslow be doing in San Francisco?' But it is you, isn't it? And you are in

San Francisco. See, George?"

She was at their table now, her eyes moving curiously from Ardith to Gavin.

"So, what are you doing in San Francisco, dear? George and I just got in from a vacation in Hawaii ourselves. Just wait until I tell Judith I ran into you and — and —" She paused, glancing at Gavin hopefully, waiting to be introduced.

"Oh, excuse me, Mrs. Prescott, may I introduce Gavin Parrish, George and Elaine Prescott, friends of my mother," Ardith managed to say smoothly.

"Gavin Parrish?" Elaine repeated slowly. Then she gasped. "You're not *the* Gavin Parrish, the one we've seen in posters around town? The pianist? Not *really!*"

"Yes, really." Gavin rose to his feet and smiled at the couple graciously.

"Well, how wonderful! How exciting!" gushed Elaine. Then she looked at Ardith. "I had no idea you knew Gavin Parrish, Ardith!" she paused significantly, waiting for an explanation.

Ardith struggled against her rising irritation. But there was no avoiding the question, so as courteously as she could, she replied.

"Gavin was a guest artist at Everett last fall."

"Oh, that's right. Your job does give you opportunity to meet celebrities. I remember dear Judith's telling us that." Elaine smiled, satisfied. "Well, now, where are you staying?"

Ardith told her.

"Well, so are we!" Elaine exclaimed. "Of course we're leaving tomorrow afternoon to go back home, but we insist you have dinner with us tonight." She rattled on before Ardith or Gavin could protest. "Now, I won't take no for an answer. Judith would never forgive us if we didn't give her a full report of what you're up to!"

Elaine giggled coquettishly, and Ardith mentally clenched her teeth against the woman's silliness. It was Gavin who rescued them.

"I'm afraid dinner tonight's impossible, Mrs. Prescott. We've made other plans," he said politely but firmly.

Her face crumpled briefly, but she quickly rallied.

"Well, cocktails anyway, in our suite. You can certainly manage that. George, what's our room number?" Silent George produced a card and an automatic silver pen from the pocket of an obviously brand new sport shirt splashed with bright Hawaiian hibiscus blossoms. He wrote down their number and handed the card to Gavin.

When the two had finally departed, Gavin groaned. "What have we let ourselves in for?"

"I'm sorry. What else could we do?" asked Ardith helplessly. "Who knows what kind of story she would take back to Florida if we hadn't at least agreed to drinks." Ardith shook her head sadly. "I'm sorry, Gavin."

"It's not your fault, darling. Look what I put you through yesterday." He patted her hand comfortingly.

"I know but —"

"Forget it, darling. Don't let it spoil our day. It certainly isn't going to spoil our evening!"

But it did. When they arrived at the Prescotts' suite, they found to their utter disappointment that the Prescotts had contacted other members of their Hawaiian tour who were still in San Francisco and had invited them also — to meet their celebrity guest, Gavin Parrish.

Ardith and Gavin telegraphed their dismay to each other several times across the room crowded with lionizing fans. But there was little either could do.

When George, bolstered into speech by more than a few cocktails, announced he had made reservations for all of them at a Fisherman's Wharf restaurant, Gavin and Ardith were swept along with the party.

Hours later, they finally made their excuses and took a taxi back to the hotel. Sitting in a quiet corner of the small lounge off the lobby, Ardith sipped hot tea while Gavin savored an espresso.

He shook his head. "I can't believe we let them steal one of our few precious evenings together."

"I feel awful, Gavin. After all, they were people I knew. At least, they were people who knew my mother. If it hadn't been for me —" Her voice trailed off wearily.

He held up his hand to ward off further apologies. "I'm too tired to argue about it. It's nobody's fault. We'll just make sure it doesn't happen again."

Secretly, Ardith worried about just what Elaine Prescott would say to her mother and Curtis about seeing her in San Francisco. And in Gavin's company! Judith knew nothing about her daughter's shipboard romance ten years ago nor of its aftermath. Ardith girded herself for the onslaught of long distance calls and queries that might come her way after Elaine returned to Key Mirador.

Well, she would just cross that bridge when she came to it.

At Ardith's door, Gavin held her close for a long while, neither of them speaking, Ardith's head against his shoulder. Then the elevator doors opened, and laughter and voices shattered the moment as a trio of couples coming from a party started along the corridor.

He kissed her lightly.

"Tomorrow we *escape*," Gavin whispered. Then he held out his hand for her key-card. She got it out of her small clutch bag and placed it in his outstretched palm. He opened her door for her.

Waiting until the merry group had passed them, Gavin stepped into Ardith's room and took her in his arms and kissed her. After a while, he loosened his hold and sighed.

"*Tomorrow!*" he said emphatically, "I promise you!"

Then he turned and started out the door. She stood in the doorway and watched him as he walked down the corridor. At the elevator he looked back, they waved, Ardith blew him a kiss, and he disappeared. Ardith went inside her room and closed the door.

Two days of their short time together already spent, she thought ruefully. But Gavin had promised *tomorrow* —

The phone by Ardith's bed awakened her, and she reached for it sleepily. A crisp, efficient voice said, "Good morning. Your room service order is on its way, ma'am."

"But I didn't order any room —" she started to say, but the caller had already hung up.

She replaced the receiver in its cradle, lay back against the lace-edged pillows, and pulled the scented sheets up over her shoulders.

They must have dialed the wrong room number, she thought.

But minutes later there was brisk knocking at her door. Puzzled, Ardith threw back the covers, slipped on her robe, and trod barefoot over the plush carpet to the door. Through the peep hole she saw a red-coated waiter with a food cart, and standing right behind him was Gavin holding a large bouquet of jonquils.

"Room service, ma'am," the waiter announced.

Ardith gave herself a quick check in the mirror. Her peach satin robe, fashioned in a Chinese style with a mandarin collar and twisted frog fasteners, looked more like an elegant dinner gown than a negligee. But her hair hung loose, a mass of dark waves tumbling over her shoulders. Giving it an ineffectual brush back with both hands, she quickly unlocked the door.

"Good morning, ma'am," the waiter said as he pulled in the cart bearing covered dishes and a large pot of coffee.

"Gavin!" Ardith exclaimed with a show of exasperation.

He smiled and stepped into the room, pausing to give her a light kiss on the cheek. "Good morning, darling!"

He tipped the waiter and waited for him to leave before he turned to Ardith. "Wanted to see how you look first thing in the morning. Now I'm satisfied. You're as beautiful as I thought you'd be!"

"You're impossible!" she declared, smiling in spite of herself. "Just how did you manage this?"

"I ordered room service, waited in the hall until they came up, then told them I'd stepped out into the hall for a minute and my door had slammed behind me."

"Gavin! That's terrible!" she remonstrated with a great show of indignation. "That's a blatant lie and an invasion of my privacy besides!"

"I thought it was rather clever," he said

with a boyish grin. "Now, my lady, break-fast is served."

"Give me a few minutes to get myself to-gether, please!" Ardith protested. "I'll be with you in a bit."

She went into the adjoining bathroom to splash her face with cold water, scrub her teeth, and brush her hair thoroughly. She started to pin it up, then shrugged and de-cided to let it go.

She found Gavin standing at the window. He had pulled back the draperies, and the sun was streaming in.

"Another glorious California day, and we're not wasting a minute of it!" he de-clared emphatically. "Come, get some coffee, and I'll tell you my plan."

Gavin poured their coffee from a silver urn and opened the serving dish for her to help herself to piping hot croissants.

"I told you last night we were going to escape today, so I've planned our getaway. I've rented a car and we're driving down the coast to Carmel."

An hour later they were in a gleaming black Porsche with red leather bucket seats, speeding down the coast highway to Carmel.

Gavin laughed and joked as they drove, seeming to love the power and freedom behind the wheel of the superbly engineered car. They were driving faster than Ardith usually felt comfortable going, but as she glanced over at Gavin, she did not want to spoil his pleasure by asking him to slow down. He looked younger than his thirty-six years with his wind-ruffled dark hair and his boyishly eager face. Every once in a while he looked over at her and grinned as if they were two school children playing hooky.

The scenery was spectacular. Ardith caught occasional glimpses of crescent-shaped beaches and wildly crashing waves on jutting rocks.

And then quite suddenly, they were in the little town of Carmel. Slowing to the minimum speed, they drove around it, marveling that it was just the way all the brochures described it — charming, picturesque, unique. Streets seemed to wind at random about trees that sidewalks accommodated. After Gavin found a parking place, they wandered for more than an hour. In a labyrinth of little streets twisting in and out of hidden courtyards, they explored out-of-the-way stores, unexpected small shops, delightful tea shops, and tiny bakeries, some looking as if they'd been built by a crew of Munchkins from Oz.

There were whole stores of just teddy bears or music boxes or leather goods, gift shops selling rare porcelains or locally crafted pottery, jewelry stores, antique clothing stores, art galleries, and book-stores. All were inviting and endlessly intriguing.

Ardith kept exclaiming over the flowers. Boxes and planters of beautiful bright blossoms of every variety were everywhere.

"I have to keep reminding myself it's December!" she said in a kind of bewildered delight.

At one point, Gavin had her wait outside a shop on a flower-boxed, brick patio while he went inside. Ardith, content to rest for a few minutes on an old-fashioned Victorian garden bench, enjoyed watching the flow of tourists in and out of the stores.

When Gavin rejoined her he was smiling with a secret. "I got to talking to the shop owner in there," he told her, "and he told me about a place where we can have lunch. It's off the beaten track a little, and it will take us about twenty minutes to drive down the coast a bit farther. But he says it's well worth it. It will be less crowded because most tourists don't know about it."

"But why did he tell you about it — a perfect stranger?"

"Maybe he just liked my face! Or thought I could be trusted with the information." He laughed, took her arm, and started back to the car. "It's for a special few, the man told me."

A weathered sign was the only clue, and they almost missed it. Driftwood Inn was down a rutted, rocky road overhung with stunted Monterey pines. Gavin inched the Porsche along. Only a few cars were parked in front of a rambling wooden building, its shingles silvered by wind and salt-heavy fog. It looked mysterious, almost foreboding, like something out of an English film.

The interior, however, had an entirely different ambiance. A dimly lit lobby led into a large, circular room that was entirely windowed. Each table, with a blue-checked cover, was placed to provide a view of the ocean. At the entry there was a bulletin board on which were hand-written comments, haikus, and bits of other poetry by customers. Gavin pointed out a sign above it that read, "Without music, life would be a mistake."

"I knew this was the right place to bring you." He smiled at Ardith, took her hand, and squeezed it.

From their table they looked out on a

scene that could have been painted by a famous seascape artist, its beauty seemed so unreal.

"Robinson Jeffers's Tor House is not far from here, the store owner told me," Gavin told Ardith. "Do you know his poetry?"

"Oh, yes," she said, "and I saw that splendid production of his *Medea* with Dame Judith Anderson on PBS. It spurred me to read his biography and buy his poetry."

"The store owner said Tor House is like something out of Camelot." Gavin paused. "Jeffers built it for his wife, Una, the enduring love of his life." Reaching across the table, Gavin took her hand in both of his. "Like you are to me. I've always loved you, you know."

A waitress came with menus, and they ordered tomatoes stuffed with shrimp and artichoke hearts. They shared a basket of crusty sourdough bread and a tiny tub of whipped butter.

"So, when are you going to make up your mind to marry me?" He looked directly at her, compelling her not to look away. "I know we've hardly had a minute to ourselves, but surely, by now, you've come to some conclusion about me — about us."

It was a moment of decision. It was the time for Ardith to tell Gavin about herself, the deep, true self.

"Gavin, there's something you need to know about me before we can make any plans," she began. "I'm a Christian."

Gavin looked puzzled. "So?" A half-smile touched his mouth.

"But if we should marry —"

Again they were interrupted by the waitress bringing their plates and refilling their coffee cups.

Gavin was frowning now. "So how does this change things for us? I've been a Christian myself since I was a teenager."

"I've made a commitment that changed me," she went on, frustrated that she was not explaining clearly. "I don't think you really understand —"

"What's there to understand? Are we talking denomination? Whatever yours is, I'll make it mine! It's that simple. Why complicate it?" Gavin started eating. As far as he was concerned, whatever Ardith thought the problem was, was solved.

"Gavin, for a committed Christian, marriage is very special," she said quietly. "It's forever and exclusive and —"

"I believe that, too, Ardith. That's why I've never married. There was never anyone else I could vow to love forever, to be faithful to — forever." He stopped, his fork halfway to his mouth. "Is it something about my past — I mean, things I may have done in the last ten years maybe — that bothers you? I'll tell you anything you want to know."

Ardith held up her hand to stop him.

"No, Gavin, don't tell me anything. I don't want to know about anything that may have happened these past few years. I didn't mean that. I —"

"Darling." Gavin moved his hand and covered hers. "Whatever I did, I never stopped loving you." His voice was low, intense, almost shaky with emotion.

He reached into his jacket pocket and brought out a small box. "The store where I made you wait outside was a jewelry store. I was looking for something specific and I found it. Let me show you."

He opened the box and held it out for her to see. It was a Mizpah coin. Then Gavin lifted one half and handed it to her.

"Remember the one we bought together on board ship? I kept mine for a long time hoping to find you and the other half. Then one day, in a fit of anger, I tossed it into the river — the Seine, as a matter of fact!" Gavin made a wry face. "I wanted to forget you and everything about our love.

"I immediately regretted it — have ever since. But now I want to replace it since we're going to be parted again. I want the Lord to watch so nothing separates us."

Tears came to Ardith's eyes as she took the gold half out of the box Gavin was holding. She smiled at him through her tears and whispered, "I still have my half."

"Well, now you have two. A whole coin, just as you have my whole heart."

They finished their lunch enjoying the magnificent view, watching some playful dolphins in the distance while the surf dashed against the jagged rocks below. Then they drove back toward Carmel.

As they reached the town center, Gavin said, "There's something else I want you to see."

They left the downtown section, and within a few minutes Gavin had pulled off onto a small side road and stopped the car.

"Here it is."

"Here what is?" Ardith asked. It looked as if they had parked in front of a tall hedge of thick bushes.

"Come along." He got out of the car, came around and opened her door, took her hand, and led her up to a gate half-hidden by the hedge. She looked up at him, puzzled.

"Go on," Gavin urged.

She lifted the latch and stepped through the gate. A few steps farther a small, rustic bridge arched over a rushing stream. The bridge ended at stone steps winding upward to a brown-shingled house with a peaked roof.

It had a lovely familiarity about it, and all at once Ardith knew why Gavin had brought her here. She looked at him, then back at the house again. It was a Swiss chalet built of dark wood with a carved balcony overhanging the entrance. It was very much like the little inn in Switzerland where they had waited in the flower-bordered courtyard for their picnic to be packed that last day they spent together long ago.

"Let's go inside," Gavin suggested softly, taking her hand.

"But —" she asked, "whose is it?"

"Ours, if we want it. A friend of mine who's in the diplomatic service in Europe owns it. He gave me use of it whenever I like, for however long I like. He may even be willing to sell it — eventually." Gavin's eyes sparkled with pleasure at her delight. "Here's the key." He took it from his pocket and handed it to her.

They walked inside. While Ardith stood in the entry hall holding her breath, Gavin went down two steps into the sunken living room and crossed to a row of French windows. He pulled open flowered drapes to reveal a bricked patio bordering a swimming pool of native stone fed by a turning water wheel.

"Come see, darling," Gavin beckoned her.

In the living room there was a corner fireplace with a hearth of blue and white hand-painted tiles. Comfortable chairs and a curved sofa circled it, and in an alcove near the windows was a baby grand piano.

"Like it?" Gavin asked.

"*Like* it? I love it. It's perfect!" Ardith exclaimed.

"Let's go upstairs," he said, leading the way up a narrow, curved stairway.

The bedroom was the same size as the living room downstairs. It was a spacious, airy room decorated in spring green and lemon yellow. The wide bed had a cushioned headboard and was upholstered in the same pattern as the polished chintz on the pale wood French provincial furniture.

Gavin drew back the filmy curtains in this room, too, and opened the glass doors onto the balcony. He took her hand and they walked outside.

All was still except for the sounds of water rushing over the rocks in the stream below and occasional bursts of bird song.

Gavin slipped his arms around her waist, and Ardith leaned back against him, resting her head on his shoulder.

"Wouldn't this be a lovely place to spend our honeymoon?" he asked.

Slowly Gavin turned Ardith around in his arms. With one movement they embraced. His mouth moved over hers searchingly, and she responded with warm eagerness.

For the first time since he had come back into her life Ardith allowed herself to enjoy fully the sensations his kiss, his nearness, brought throbbingly alive in her. For the first time she admitted to herself what this man meant to her, what she felt in his embrace. She wanted what she felt to go on and on.

The transforming power of love was coursing through her again, thawing the frozen regions of her heart.

"My darling," Gavin murmured over and over as he kissed her mouth, her cheeks, her forehead, her closed eyelids, then her mouth again. "I love you so terribly. Say you love me, too."

"I do, Gavin. I do love you!"

"If you only knew how long I've waited to hear you say that," he whispered as he gathered her closer, holding her so tightly against him she could feel his heart thudding.

Their lips met again, this time in a kiss of such sweetness and depth it brought tears to Ardith's eyes. It was a wordless commitment, in which everything was said, everything promised.

Suddenly the telephone's piercing ring broke the intimate moment.

They broke apart, startled.

"The phone!" Ardith gasped. "I didn't realize it was connected."

The phone rang once more, and Ardith asked, "Should you answer it?"

"I'm trying to decide." Gavin frowned.

"But if your friend's in Europe —"

"He is, of course, but the number is a working one." He paused. "It could be for me."

"But who would know you're here?"

"I've often spent weekends here when I've been on tour on the West Coast —"

"But who would know we came here today?" she persisted.

The phone kept ringing.

"Only Renay. I always let her know where I'll be in case anything should come up, like now, with these contracts pending —" He hesitated. Then as the phone rang again, he said, "I guess I'd better answer it."

He walked to pick up the phone beside the bed, and although Ardith could not hear what he was saying, the tone of the conversation seemed as brusque as it was brief.

Gavin came back out on the balcony. His artistic fingers stretched taut, then clenched tightly.

"That was Renay," he told her shortly. "She took a chance we'd end up here. She's here in Carmel with the sponsor's agent for the Australian part of our tour. He's flying back to Melbourne tonight, and the papers have to be signed today."

He put his arms on Ardith's shoulder, drew her close, and rested his chin on her head. "I'm so sorry. It's one of those totally unpredictable things. Otherwise Renay wouldn't have intruded on our day together."

Ardith was not so sure the interruption wasn't intentional. But she hid her disappointment as well as her suspicions about Renay's motives. And when Renay arrived at the little house, Ardith tried to quell her rising resentment.

But when she met Renay's cool glance, she felt a surge of pure jealousy. Renay was superbly outfitted in what Ardith had come to call California-chic, in a toast raw silk blazer, a cream silk blouse, narrow cream wool pants, and high heels. Unexpected hostility surged like a tropical storm in Ardith and was just as difficult to control. Fortunately, her introduction to the stocky, freckled Australian distracted her.

Meanwhile, Renay hardly acknowledged her presence and immediately started explaining to Gavin the new terms of the contract. Ardith took a magazine and went upstairs to wait on the balcony until their meeting was over.

Her random magazine choice failed to hold her interest, and after she had looked at it cover to cover and read one or two of its articles, the conference downstairs was still going on.

Restless, Ardith took the outside stairway from the balcony to the terrace and from there out to the yard and gate. She decided she would go for a walk. She had noticed the gravel road went straight down to the beach.

In case the meeting finished suddenly

and Gavin came looking for her, she scribbled a note on the back of one of her deposit slips from her pocket checkbook and left it sticking out of the magazine on one of the canvas deck chairs.

The beach was nearly deserted in the late afternoon shadows, and she walked for a while until she found a protected place to sit and watch the sunset. She tried to clear her mind of all the negative feelings Renay's peremptory arrival had spawned.

If she became part of Gavin's demanding life, such interruptions, meetings, and unscheduled conferences would be commonplace. And Renay, too, would be a part of Gavin's professional life. It was foolish to feel resentful, jealous, because his agent happened to be an attractive, sophisticated woman. If the agent had been a man, someone like Hans Friedborg, wouldn't she still have resented the intrusion into their brief, beautiful moment?

Yes, she would have, but maybe not quite so much! Ardith had to smile at her own irrationality.

The sun was touching the sea with a dazzling brilliance now. Out nearly to the horizon she saw two surfers, gliding and waiting for the special wave.

Gradually Ardith began to feel at peace

as she watched the sun plunge into the sea, a circle of bright orange immersing in the shimmering purple water.

"So, here you are! I thought you'd run away from me." Gavin's voice spoke behind her, and she turned just as he crouched down beside her. He placed his arm around her shoulder, leaned over, and kissed her upturned mouth.

"After Renay and that Aussie left, I didn't find your note right away. I called, and when you didn't answer, I panicked! I thought I'd lost you. Don't ever scare me like that again. Don't ever leave me like that!" he demanded, and just as demandingly he kissed her.

"I won't!" she replied, but her words were blown away on the wind.

It was late when they drove back to San Francisco. They didn't talk much on the way because it took all of Gavin's concentration to drive through the heavy fog.

Chapter Eleven

"Let's not go anywhere New Year's Eve," Gavin had said. "There are several parties. Renay's having one at her apartment on Russian Hill, and I'm tempted to go just to show you off! But I'd rather have you all to myself our last night together."

His words had struck a responsive chord in Ardith. It would be their last night together. Her days in San Francisco had sped like a dream and she would be leaving the next day to fly back to North Carolina, to Everett and her life there.

But Ardith knew her life would never be the same again. For the second time Gavin had changed her forever.

Late New Year's Eve afternoon as Ardith dressed for their last evening together, she realized the importance of the hours ahead. It would be the last opportunity they would have to talk seriously about the future. There were still things to be discussed, to be understood between them.

Ardith had saved her favorite and the most extravagant of all her new dresses to wear this special night. But when she zipped herself into the flame-colored Georgette with the beaded yoke and looked in the mirror, suddenly it did not seem the right thing after all.

She took it off and tossed it aside, thought for a minute, then changed into black velvet pants. With it she tried on the ivory silk blouse she had impulsively bought on her first day in California. Hand-painted with a spray of golden poppies across it from shoulder to waist, it seemed perfect for her last evening in San Francisco.

She brushed her hair into a lustrous swirl, fastening it with tortoise shell combs. Then she put on the blue cloisonné earrings in the shape of butterflies, bought on their day in Chinatown, and headed for Gavin's room.

When Gavin saw her, he confirmed her choice. With both hands he framed her face and kissed her. "You look absolutely stunning! You are so beautiful," he said huskily, gazing at her with tender seriousness as though he were memorizing her face.

He drew her to him, his arms holding her tightly. "How am I going to get through the next ten months without you?" They stood motionless for a long moment before he released her and exclaimed, "No, I'm not going to start out the evening with doom and gloom! This is New Year's Eve — a time to be happy, to look forward to the future. Our future!" Gavin smiled. "Right?"

"Right!" Ardith attempted to smile over the hot tightness in her throat.

"And I have a present for you! A sort of late Christmas present, an early birthday, or whatever." He went over to the couch where a beautifully wrapped box lay. He brought it back and laid it in her arms.

It was rectangular in shape and very light.

Ardith fingered the bow and looked at Gavin speculatively. "It looks so pretty I hate to tear the paper," she said slowly, as she carefully started to unwrap it.

"It's prettier inside. Hurry, open it!" Gavin urged. His eyes shining with excitement, he was as anxious as a little boy to see how she liked his present.

Ardith noticed the name of a famous furrier on the lid of the box as she lifted it. Then as she pushed aside the layers of tissue, she saw the pale, creamy lushness of an umber mink jacket.

"Oh, Gavin, no! I couldn't!" Ardith was awed.

"Try it on," he commanded, taking it from her shaking hands and holding it out for her.

"Oh, Gavin, I couldn't accept something like this!"

"Of course you can. Here, slip it on."

She felt the unbelievable warmth, the lightness, the luxurious texture as it went over her shoulders and caressed her neck.

"It's perfect!" he declared, stepping back to admire.

"Gavin, dear, it's much too expensive a gift for you to give me," Ardith said quietly as she removed the jacket.

Gavin looked puzzled and hurt. "Why not? I don't understand."

"Just take my word for it. I can't accept it."

"I would have bought you a ring, but I was afraid you wouldn't accept *that*." Gavin flung out his hands in frustration.

Ardith didn't answer. Her hand smoothed the fur thoughtfully, almost regretfully, as she returned the jacket to its box.

"Would you have taken a ring?" Gavin demanded. "Are we going to be married?"

A discreet knock at the suite's door prevented Ardith's reply.

Gavin clenched his jaw. "I've ordered

dinner up here. I wanted to ensure our not being disturbed our last evening together."

Two red-coated waiters rolled in the cart, then deftly transferred its cloth, napkins, silver, and glassware onto a table before the large window and its view of the city.

Gavin walked over to the piano, lifted the lid, and trailed his hands along the keys, making a few impatient trills. When the two waiters had left, he whirled around from the piano and faced Ardith.

"Well! I'm waiting for an answer. Are you going to marry me?"

Hands clasped together, she stood looking at the tall man confronting her, and suddenly her heart was gripped with love, compassion, and longing.

She loved him, would never love anyone else, no matter what.

She began to tremble. Then she nodded. She held out her arms, hands open, palms up, and said, "Yes! Oh, Gavin, yes!"

In a moment he was by her side.

He looked at her for a long time before he took her hands and slowly drew them up and around his neck, holding them there with his.

"You mean that?" he asked solemnly.

"Yes, I mean it," she answered.

He shook his head slowly as if in wonder.

"Do you have any idea how happy you've made me?"

He did not wait for an answer but brought her hands down to his lips and kissed them. Taking the left one, he ran his fingers down her ring finger and said softly, "When we're married you can't stop me, and I'm going to cover you with jewels, smother you with furs." He threw back his head and laughed. "Oh, my darling! We're going to be so happy! Now, we can really celebrate the New Year! I've got something special to toast our new life together and to welcome in this memorable New Year."

He walked over to the table where the waiter had placed a bucket of ice and drew out a long-necked bottle.

"Before you resist," he said, holding up one hand to her in warning, "this is something new from the beautiful vineyards in the Napa Valley — I wish we had time to drive up there. But we will someday. Anyway, it's sparkling grape juice, nonalcoholic and perfectly delicious. I've already tasted it!"

He opened it with great ceremony, poured the glistening pale gold liquid with its tiny bursting silver bubbles into tall tulip-shaped glasses, and handed one to Ardith.

"To us!" he said, touching the delicate edge of his glass to hers to make a high tinkling sound.

Ardith took a sip. Its icy tartness made her eyes water. "Oh, my! That is delicious!" she murmured.

Gavin leaned forward and kissed her on the mouth. His lips were cold and tasted of grapes.

"I love you," he said with great solemnity.

"And I love you," she replied, knowing she meant it with all her heart.

"Now, let's eat! The chef promised to outdo himself," Gavin declared, leading her to the window table and holding out her chair.

As she seated herself, Gavin began lifting the heavy covers from a gourmet feast: lobster, duck à l'orange with almonds, wild rice, and petits pois in cream sauce, and for dessert, a lime chiffon pie with a chocolate crust and rich, dark Hawaiian Kona coffee.

During dinner they talked about their week together, recalling the places they had been and what they had enjoyed most. They even laughed about the appearance of the Prescotts and that disastrous evening.

"I'm going to live on this for the next few months," Gavin told her. "I only wish you were going with me. Just think of going to the Orient together. Doesn't shopping in Hong Kong or spending a weekend at a Japanese country inn with a view of Fujiyama tempt you? We could go tomorrow to get a license, see about your passport —"

"Stop, Gavin. You're tempting me!" Ardith put a restraining hand on his arm. "But I have a contract at Everett, you know." She shook her head regretfully.

Gavin sighed. "I know. When we're married we will travel — but differently, not the rush, rush of airports and schedules. I've always wanted to take a cruise of the Alaskan waterways —" he said. They began to make lovers' plans, sharing their dreams and hopes.

After they had finished their coffee, Gavin led Ardith back to the couch, his arm around her waist. They sat down close together, her head resting on his shoulder. His hand stroked her hair, and he loosened the pins that held her coiled knot. His fingers tangled in her hair as it fell. Then his hand gently circled her neck and slowly turned her head toward him. Very deliberately he began to kiss her.

Ardith eagerly responded. She closed her eyes, then felt his kisses on her eyelids, heard the soft tenderness of his voice whispering things she could not quite hear but understood from his tone of voice.

She felt weightless, drifting, soothed by the warm sweetness of her feelings, moving effortlessly out on a current, riding a tide that was drawing her farther and farther —

Then she heard Gavin speaking urgently. "Darling, stay with me here tonight. I want you so much. I need you. We've waited so long. We'll be apart so long —" His voice was pleading, reassuring. "I love you so much. I know you feel the same way. If you really love me —"

Somehow those words awakened her from the mesmerizing sensation in which she was floating without seeming to have the strength or will to move. *If you really love me —*

Those words were the same that Annalee's young boyfriend Ken had used. *He said if I really loved him I would —*

Annalee's troubled little face invaded Ardith's love-clouded mind.

She stirred in Gavin's arms, gently disentangling herself, and stood up to go. If she had given in to their youthful passion in Switzerland ten years ago, would anything have been different? If she gave into that passion now, how would it change their relationship?

"Darling, please." Gavin's voice was low, tender. He reached out and caught her hand, gently tugging to bring her back beside him.

But Ardith moved away, gathering up her hair and straightening her shoulders. Without turning back, she said firmly, "No, Gavin, we mustn't — we can't —"

He rose, came up behind her, circled her waist with his arms, then spun her around, holding her with his hands.

"But why not?" he demanded fiercely. "We love each other, don't we? Whom would we hurt? We're going to be married! Don't tell me you believe saying a few words before a minister or a judge, some figurehead, makes that much difference?"

"Yes, I do," Ardith said quietly, "because we will be saying those few words before God, asking him to bless those vows, help us to keep them. Then we'll be truly married, committed to each other."

Gavin dropped his hands, plunging them angrily into his jacket pockets. "I couldn't feel more married, more committed to you than I do now, Ardith. I love you. You say you love me. That's enough for me!"

Ardith put out a hand toward him. "Please, try to understand, Gavin."

"I *am* trying to understand."

There was a long pause.

"So — because I do love you — I'll respect your reasons even if I don't agree with them," he said finally.

Then he walked over to the piano and sat down. In another minute he started playing. At first, in strident notes of strength and fire, the intensity of his playing reflected the storm in his heart. The Grieg concerto echoed the deep longing, the fierce aching within them both to belong fully to each other.

Gradually the quality of the music changed, became reflective, romantic, softer, less turbulent.

Ardith looked over at his strong profile — his head flung back, his eyes closed, his hands moving purposefully, striking each note with clarity and strength.

Ardith's very soul was touched by the beauty of his music. She moved quietly across the thick carpet to stand in the bow of the piano. Gavin, as if conscious of her presence, opened his eyes and held hers in a close, intimate, tender look. It was as if the two of them were alone in the world, enveloped in the music, the dream of love, an exchange as deep and mystical as their mutual promise.

Continuing to play with one hand, he held out the other one, and she went and sat beside him on the bench until he had finished.

Outside, the fog had enveloped the city so that the lights below were blurs of color. The view from the window seemed to seal them into a grayed, unreal softness. It was a long time before either of them moved or spoke.

Later, much later, sitting side by side on the sofa, Gavin's arms around her, her head on his shoulder, they made their plans.

"Ten months seems a lifetime," Gavin lamented.

"I know, but we'll both be busy. It will pass —" She tried to sound optimistic.

"You have the key to the house now. We'll meet there in September. If for any reason things change, for either one of us —" He paused and held her tightly. "— Not that they will. Not for me at least —"

"Or for me!" she protested mildly.

"We need to have that clause in our contract," he said to her facetiously. "But if something should happen to change your mind, then simply don't come."

"Oh, Gavin, I'll be there — in that lovely little house! I'll be dreaming of it all the time." At midnight they heard the whistles in the city proclaim the new year under the muffling fog.

"Next year we'll be celebrating a new year together," Gavin reminded her at the door of her suite. Then he cupped her chin with his hand and kissed her. "How will I ever get through the next ten months without you?"

"With God's help," she said softly, smiling through her tears and gently returning his kiss.

Chapter Twelve

Ardith was putting the last few articles in her suitcase when she heard a knock at her door. Assuming it was Gavin, she called out, "Be there in a minute, darling!"

But when she opened it Renay Evans stood in the hall instead.

"Sorry to disappoint you," she said archly.

Wearing a lynx-collared and cuffed rust suede coat and high-heeled boots, Renay sauntered into the room, and then pivoting like a model she turned to Ardith.

"Are you ready?" she asked.

"Almost," Ardith answered, glancing at her wrist watch. "But Gavin said the limousine wouldn't be here until —"

"Oh, that's been changed. I'm driving you to the airport," Renay said casually.

"But Gavin —"

"I set up two important press interviews for him for this afternoon. If he went with you, he wouldn't be back in time to make them. They're special ones. He can't turn them down. One is for the Sunday supplement of the San Francisco *Chronicle*; the other's a personality profile *Celebrity Magazine*'s been wanting to do. Since we're leaving —" Renay shrugged as if that settled the matter. Dismay, disappointment, suspicion, and anger converged in Ardith. Had Renay set these up on purpose?

So that Renay would not see her reaction, Ardith turned back to her packing. She bit her lip hard to keep her emotions from betraying her in front of Renay's smug and total control. Try as she might, Ardith could not like her. There was such a hardness about the woman.

Two minutes later Gavin arrived, frustrated and furious, striding into the room after a quick knock. He had come for a few last minutes alone with Ardith.

"You've heard?" he demanded. He put his tensed hands on Ardith's shoulders and looked at her with flashing dark eyes. "Renay tried to arrange some other time, but they both claimed immovable deadlines." He pulled her close, cradling her head against his shoulders. "You'd think we could at least have this last day together without some kind of blasted interruption —"

"I'll wait in the lobby for you, Ardith," Renay's voice informed her coolly.

There was only a little time left for them to say all those foolish, tender, loving, last-minute things to each other, for a few lingering kisses, for promises to write often.

Gavin pressed her hands to his lips. "Remember, Carmel in September!" It was like a lovely song title, Ardith thought as she stepped into the elevator. And yet, it had a frighteningly familiar ring — Carmel in September! Paris in September! Ten years ago that promise had been her talisman, and then — The similarity suddenly chilled her. It wouldn't happen again. It couldn't! *We love each other,* she thought. *Nothing can go wrong this time.*

"The Lord watch between me and thee while we are absent from each other," she repeated over and over.

Then the elevator doors slid open at the lobby, and Ardith found Renay sitting opposite them, waiting for her.

"My car's at the side entrance." She directed the bellhop carrying Ardith's bags.

The day was gray and chill. Fog hung in misty, drifting wisps as they left the hotel in Renay's low-slung red Corvette. Gone was all the glorious sunshine. Gone were all the golden days she had spent with Gavin.

Renay expertly threaded through midafternoon city traffic and out to the freeway. They did not speak until they were speeding toward the airport in the fast lane. It was Renay who broke the uneasy silence that had settled between them.

"I was surprised not to find you in Gavin's suite this morning — or him in yours!"

Ardith, jolted by her remark, turned to stare at her.

Renay shrugged. "Well, you needn't act so shocked. It would have been unrealistic for me to think anything else. After all, Gavin's told me about your *teenage* romance, how you lost track of each other, and in some kind of phenomenal coincidence met again last fall." She gave a short, unpleasant laugh. "And to think I was the one to arrange his substitution for that sick soprano at your college!"

Ardith said nothing. She was too appalled at Renay's tactlessness.

"So, what are you holding out for? Marriage? You've been married once, I know. So, why didn't you sleep with Gavin?"

Ardith felt her face flame as anger welled hotly within her. Her hands clenched convulsively, but she told herself not to stoop to Renay's level by defending herself.

Even though her heart was hammering

and she felt deeply offended, she answered in a steady voice. "Because I believe marriage is a sacred vow. I wanted — we both wanted to wait until we could plan a church wedding, take —"

"You've got to be kidding!" Renay interrupted her. "That couldn't be Gavin's idea! He's the most impatient person I know. Wait for a *wedding!* I know him too well to believe *that!*"

Ardith said nothing more. She felt Renay glance at her a couple of times curiously in the ensuing silence. Then Renay spoke in a voice tinged heavily with sarcasm. "Don't tell me you're a *Christian?*"

The unmistakable ridicule in the question shook Ardith more than the bluntness of the inquiry itself. For a moment she was speechless. Then sending up a swift prayer, *Lord, let me be a good witness; don't let me blow it,* Ardith answered quietly, "Yes, I am."

As if she had been waiting for something like this to set her off, Renay exploded.

"I can't believe I'm hearing this! It's incredible to me that Gavin could be attracted to someone like you! I've been with him for nearly three years. I know him. Have you any idea what it would be like to be married to someone like Gavin Parrish?

"I know Gavin better than he knows himself. He's living out some kind of fantasy with you, a revival of an old romantic musical on Broadway — nice enough, but outdated." She talked on in staccato spurts, emphasizing her points with a kid-gloved fist on the steering wheel.

"I know the whole man — the complicated, dedicated, self-centered, temperamental artist — the selfish, ambitious person he really is. He would sacrifice anything and anyone to his career!"

Even as she wove in and out of traffic, Renay never stopped talking until she had pulled up to the concrete apron outside the airport.

Ardith started to get out of the car, but Renay grabbed her arm and held her back. Her face was very close, so close Ardith could see the intense anger in the large, brown, expertly decorated eyes.

"Listen to me. It may save you a lot of grief if you pay attention. In spite of his temporary passion for you, music is his only mistress. You can't compete with what he gets from music — the adulation, attention, the applause! You can't give him round-the-clock adoration!

"Don't be a fool, Ardith! Gavin may think he wants you, but if you go ahead and marry him, you'll regret it!"

A redcap peered in at the window of the car. "Your baggage ma'am? Which flight?"

"I have to go!" Ardith said in a choked voice, tugging her arm from Renay's grasp.

"Just remember what I'm telling you. It would be a terrible mistake to marry Gavin!"

Badly shaken but unwilling to let Renay know how badly, Ardith spoke in a calm, steady voice. "Well, that's up to Gavin to decide."

With that she opened the car door and stepped out. Without looking back, she walked through the glass doors into the huge terminal.

It was not until she had checked in for her flight and found a seat in the passenger lounge that her reaction came. She felt almost ill. There had been so much spite, so much venom in the things Renay had said. But had there also been some truth?

Ardith's head started to ache. She went into a restroom, found two aspirin in her purse, filled a paper cup with water, and swallowed them.

She looked at her pale reflection in the mirror above the sink. Her eyes looked large and haunted.

Then she heard her flight number called

on the PA system, echoing in the tiled room. She turned away from the stricken face and walked quickly down the corridor to her plane.

Back at Everett, Ardith felt winter had come with dramatic suddenness. Or maybe it was just the bleak contrast with California that assailed her. The campus looked drab with the trees bare and the ground hard and brown under patches of snow. The whole eastern part of the country was gripped in record cold, and while Gavin's letters from Australia told of ninety degree temperatures and sunny beaches, North Carolina shivered.

The first few weeks after she returned, Ardith was inundated with flowers and telegrams and calls from Gavin. Her first day back at Bower House a huge bouquet of spring flowers — purple irises, yellow jonquils, and blue Michaelmas daisies — was delivered. These were followed by a dewy fresh lei of gardenias flown from Hawaii by Gavin as he started his tour.

Although his notes were short, they were filled with words of love, telling her how much he missed her, how he longed to see her, how he wished she were with him.

In spite of his reassurances, every time

she opened a florist's box or read one of his notes, she remembered the conversation with Renay on the way to the San Francisco International Airport. She could imagine Renay's voice clearly. *He doesn't need someone like you! What could you do for him? He needs someone like me fending for him, tough enough to handle what he can't handle himself. Musicians aren't fit for the real world! They have to have someone who is — and you're certainly not it!*

A continual contradiction stormed in Ardith's mind and heart. Maybe, they were too different. Maybe it wouldn't work!

But we love each other!

Love? Did they have the right kind of love for each other, the kind of love the Bible described? Or was it — as Renay had suggested — a "temporary passion" that would disappear as soon as it was satisfied?

As January merged into February, her days with Gavin in San Francisco became as hard to remember as the warmth of spring. Ardith really had to try to remember her walks with Gavin along the holiday-decorated streets —

She found it more and more difficult to recall the crisp, sunny days when the smell of fog, imported coffee, and the distinctive perfumes of stylish shoppers mingled with the sea wind off the bay. The impressions of San Francisco slowly faded — the glitter of expensive gifts, the exotic sights, the smells of Chinatown and "North Beach," espresso in a small Italian coffee house, the night dazzle of the city from the Top of the Mark, the street flower vendors, and a cluster of fragrant violets pinned to her coat.

It was even hard to picture Gavin's face, looking at her with eyes of love, unless she concentrated. Those days seemed like a golden dream, shriveling into grayed memories in the bone-chilling wind that swept snow down from the mountains.

One day shortly after her return from California, Ardith ran into Annalee on campus. Their exchange was brief because Annalee was on her way to class and a freezing wind whipped about them. At Ardith's prompting, Annalee recounted the details of her Christmas holidays.

"Well, it was an incredible hassle during the holidays! I told my parents we were going skiing — together! Just the two of us! My mother went to bed with a migraine, and my dad stormed out of the house. Then they both nailed me the next day, demanding I have Ken come and face them.

"And then —" She paused, shaking her

long blond hair as if in disbelief. "— They suggested we get *married!*

"Well, Ken was blown away. He turned white as a sheet, but he kept his cool and told my father he'd have to think about it.

"Anyway, since we'd already made the arrangements, we went skiing. We decided we were over eighteen and adults and — well," Annalee sighed, "You're not going to believe this, Mrs. Winslow, but the first day on the slopes Ken broke his leg!" She paused again dramatically, then rushed on. "Of course, he landed in the hospital, and that was the end of our romantic weekend!"

"Now what?" asked Ardith, trying to suppress her urge to laugh.

Annalee shrugged. "Oh, I don't know! Neither of us is really ready for *marriage.* Ken's still on crutches, and we've both got a lot of studying to do right now — and a lot of thinking!"

As Ardith walked on, her head bent against the fierce wind, she could not help thinking, *God works in mysterious ways.*

Immediately Ardith applied that thought to her own trip to San Francisco. God had provided several ways to protect her from going against her beliefs. She remembered how close she had come to succumbing to

her physical desires. The interruptions —
the unexpected meeting with the Prescotts,
Renay's precipitous arrival with the Australian agent at the little house in Carmel,
the concert, Gavin's interviews — all had
interfered with their opportunities to be
alone.

Were all these incidents just happen-
stance? Or were they purposely ordained?
A loving Father's care?

Ardith was convinced there was a divine
plan that had prevented what might, in the
worldly view of things, be considered the
natural outcome of a relationship between
two "consenting adults."

Thinking of Annalee's experience,
Ardith decided to search in her Bible for
God's plan for her. As she had done before, she would read — search — until she
recognized that passage that spoke to her
need.

But before she had had a chance to
pursue that intention two things happened
simultaneously that made her more uneasy
and indecisive about her promise to Gavin.

Gavin had put her on the mailing list to
receive his publicity notices from a clip-
ping service he employed, and early in
March, Ardith began to receive bulging
manilla envelopes filled with newspaper

accounts, critiques, and articles about Gavin and his tour. Among favorable reviews by various music critics on the concerts themselves, there were also pictures and items from society pages and gossip columns. The service clipped and sent anything in which Gavin's name was printed.

Ardith understood that attending social events such as charity balls, receptions, and benefits was part of the whole tour package. But was being seen at discos and poolside parties of the rich and socially prominent also required?

At almost the same time, she was passing a magazine rack at a local drugstore when she happened to see a full-color portrait of Gavin on the cover of the latest issue of *Celebrity*. The blurb underneath promised an explosive interview with the well-known concert pianist.

Ardith had never bought or read the magazine, but this time of course would be an exception. She added it to her purchases and hurried home to read the article.

When she had finished reading it and put it aside, she wished she had not.

An explanatory note stated that the interview had been taped while Gavin was in

San Francisco before leaving on an extended Far East tour and that it had been "edited" before printing. The article itself was written in the laid-back style characteristic of the magazine, with only a few direct quotations from Gavin.

For the most part the article was complimentary, lauding Gavin's talent and his musical accomplishments. But the depiction of him as a "typical eighties bachelor, a connoisseur of wine, women, and wheels, with a penchant to live in the fast lane" disturbed Ardith.

To a question about his personal philosophy, Gavin supposedly had replied,

"I don't have time to spend thinking of how I live my life — I just live it to the fullest and do what I enjoy most with the people I like best."

"*What kind of people are those?*"

"Amusing people, witty people! I like to be distracted, have a good time, after spending five or six hours at the piano. I like to laugh, have fun. After all, what's life all about anyway?"

Mechanically Ardith repeated the quotation. *What's life all about anyway?* Had Gavin really said that? Was that how he really felt?

Her ringing phone interrupted her perplexing thoughts. It was Dean Craddock. As the head of the Cultural Arts Program at Everett, he had made up the list of visiting lecturers and artists who would be appearing during the next college year.

"I think we need to go over the list together, Mrs. Winslow, and make out a tentative schedule so we can have everything ready for the fall semester."

Next fall! Suddenly Ardith realized that when she met Gavin in Carmel in September, she might not be returning to Everett or to Bower House next fall. *When* she met Gavin? Did she mean *if?*

"Could you come to my office next Thursday for a conference?" Dean Craddock's request demanded an immediate response.

Quickly Ardith collected her scattered thoughts. "Next Thursday, yes, of course, Dean Craddock. What time?"

As soon as she had hung up Ardith knew she had to begin her Bible study before her appointment with Dean Craddock because the subject of her contract for the next year at Everett would come up and she would have to tell him whether she planned to stay.

The thought of making such an imminent and binding decision terrified her. Saying she would not be back at Everett next fall meant she was going blindly into the unknown. Ardith knew she needed help reaching the decision.

Fortunately she was free to begin studying the next morning. Her mind was a jumble of conflicting thoughts as she opened her Bible and began to read.

The night before she had reread the *Celebrity* profile of Gavin, then stayed awake long into the night, going over what it had said and reading between the lines.

She knew that often such magazine pieces were more fiction than fact, that the writer could project an image by the manipulation of a few words. The slick, hedonistic man the article portrayed was not the Gavin she had come to know. He certainly was not the man she loved. What if she were as mistaken about Gavin as she had been about Tedo?

All the possibilities crowded in on her. Maybe she would be trading a comfortable, tranquil, comparatively carefree life for one of turmoil and misery. Maybe she had misled Gavin. Maybe she could never adjust to his life. But then, maybe God was asking her to give up her safety and seclusion at Everett.

She turned to her Bible deciding that now was the time to trust God for direction. Every morning she would spend at least an hour praying, seeking the Lord's direction.

By Thursday her heart was at peace. Each day Proverbs 3:6 had seemed to speak to her need: "In all your ways acknowledge him, and he shall direct your paths." Each day it became clearer to Ardith that it was time to trust God and move out in faith.

Gavin was back in her life for a reason. If the reason was that they would start a new life together, then she must cut her ties at Everett.

She remembered something her grandmother had told her when she went to Sunnyfields broken in spirit after Tedo's accident. Ardith had felt she would never recover, and her grandmother, who had known much tragedy in her own life, told her gently, "Nothing is forever. And thank God for that. We travel on beyond the next hill, and that may be the best part of all."

With sudden clarity Ardith knew that was right.

At eighteen she had felt the pain of the heartbreak in Paris would never end. But it had eventually. Even her guilt-ridden grief over Tedo had gradually faded.

With God's help, she would survive again if Gavin was not there when she got to Carmel, or even if he came and they found the separation had proved they were not meant for each other after all. But at least she ought to go and find out.

That afternoon she walked across campus already beginning to stir with slight signs of spring. A faint aura of green seemed to hover over the bare branches, and here and there a brave crocus thrust a tentative shoot through the frozen ground. Ardith's heart lifted.

She entered Dean Craddock's office and looked around her with satisfaction. The room was furnished with a mixture of fine period pieces, donated or willed to the college by its principal benefactors, the Everett family. Handsome antiques mingled with modern comfort. There were deep leather sofas and chairs, brass lamps, and over the paneled fireplace an impressive oil portrait of the first president of the college in 1856.

While she waited for Dean Craddock, Ardith recalled her last meeting in this office. Then she hadn't dreamed that there would be a last-minute change in the guest artist and that Gavin Parrish would come back into her life.

When Dean Craddock was free to see her, Ardith went into the inner office to tell him of her plan to resign. Dismayed, he begged her to reconsider. He had come to rely on Ardith for a great deal. He knew it would be difficult to find someone as reliable and competent to replace her.

"Perhaps your plans will change," he suggested.

"Even if they do, Dean Craddock, I believe it's time for me to make a change," Ardith said firmly. As she said the words, she felt a little flutter of fear in the pit of her stomach. Quickly she thrust away the nagging apprehension.

Easter was early in April, and Everett would close for a two-week spring vacation, which Ardith would spend at Sunnyfields.

Good Friday afternoon, as she put her bags in the trunk of her car to leave for Melrose, the chapel bell began to ring. The bell traditionally tolled out thirty-three strokes, the number of years of Christ's life on earth, at the hour of his death on the cross.

Ardith stood still in reverent meditation until the last stroke echoed out across the campus.

The afternoon seemed to darken slightly with rain-filled clouds as Ardith drove across the nearly deserted campus and out through the twin stone pillars on either side of the gate.

As she neared the expressway turn-off that led to Sunnyfields, the countryside became all sunshine and spring bloom. Her grandmother's garden would be at its best. The azaleas would be rosy flames against the dark, waxy green of the camellia bushes, and the air would be fragrant with the softness of spring.

Ardith's mild melancholy disappeared. It would be good to be with Charlotte, to bask in the serenity and peace of this special place. Ardith longed for it as she never had before, after her long, lonely winter.

Chapter Thirteen

The summer, Ardith discovered, was long and lonely, too. Although she had not planned to, she spent most of it alone at the house at Seawood Beach.

This year her time at Sunnyfields was not the restful, restorative interlude she looked forward to after the busy life at Everett. Her grandmother's concern about Ardith's plans was apparent every time Ardith mentioned Gavin. It became verbal one day when Ardith shared part of a letter from Gavin in which he spoke of tentative plans for another tour to Australia and New Zealand the following year and another to the Philippines and Japan.

"And if you marry, would you go with him?" Charlotte asked.

Ardith hesitated. "I don't know. Anyway, it's not definite."

Charlotte raised her eyebrows. "Not definite? Do you mean the marriage or the tour?"

"The tour, of course," she said quickly, flushing at the sharpness of both her grandmother's eyes and tone of voice. "He really hates it, you know, all the traveling —"

"Then why does he go on?" demanded her grandmother. "Isn't he successful enough by now? What drives him? Certainly he can afford to take more time off between concerts. He surely doesn't have to grasp for each chance to play like some beginner who needs publicity." Ardith had no answers to those questions. Indeed, she had asked them herself many times before, and Gavin's letters gave her no clue of his true feelings. Sometimes they seemed written at a peak of elation over the reception of an audience and the good reviews. Other times they were heavy with depression, loneliness, boredom, and weariness of the constant travel and the crowds. In fact, she found his letters often inconsistent in everything but his repeated protestation of his love and longing for her.

For the first time she could remember, Ardith felt a sense of relief when she left Sunnyfields to drive to the beach. She had always been so close to her grandmother that now Charlotte's anxiety and the concern in her eyes seemed to echo Ardith's own apprehensions. And Ardith did not, at this point, need anyone else's anxieties increasing her own.

At the first sight of the sea and the

slanted roof of her cottage behind the dunes, Ardith felt a glad sense of home-coming. The little house, bleached by the sun and sea wind to the color of sand and driftwood, was very special. Her father's legacy to her, it was a place of healing and spiritual refreshment.

The screened-in porch looked out on the beach and ocean, and she often took her meals there. Inside it was small, but the uncluttered floors and few pieces of furniture made the dwelling seem bigger.

Although she had brought her water-colors and drawing paper and all the books she had not had time to read during her busy winter, she ended up spending most of her time walking along the ocean's edge, swimming, and shell-hunting in the sunny days, and listening to tapes of Gavin's music at night.

It was the music that made her feel closest to him as the memories of actually being with him became less real. She had come to depend more and more on his correspondence, but although she had left forwarding addresses at both Everett and Sunnyfields, Gavin's letters came less and less frequently. Once a flooding stream, they had dwindled to a mere trickle of hastily written notes. By mid-August they had stopped altogether.

Maybe with characteristic impatience Gavin had felt writing a waste of time since they would soon be together. Still, not hearing from him heightened Ardith's apprehension.

After Labor Day most of the summer crowd left and Ardith rarely saw anyone when she walked the beach. September 10, the date of her departure for California drew near, and as it approached all her old doubts and uncertainties stirred again.

Why had she not heard from Gavin? Had he changed his mind about meeting her? No! Ardith was sure that Gavin would keep to their agreement. She reread his most recent letter, written weeks ago, and reassured herself. He was eagerly looking forward to their rendezvous in Carmel.

The last muggy night before she was to leave, Ardith could not sleep. After an especially hot day, there was no wind, and the ocean lay shimmering like a sheet of glass in the moonlight. She walked out onto the porch to get a breath of air and stared out at the sea. Was Gavin flying over another ocean now back to the States?

A pall of depression weighed on her as heavily as the lingering heat of the day. She put on one of Gavin's tapes and listened to the sweet, sad strains of Beethoven's "Sonata" as she paced back and forth in the moonlight, quoting the verse from Joshua that had helped her last September: "Be strong and of good courage; do not be afraid, nor be dismayed, for the Lord your God is with you wherever you go."

At the end of the week, even though there had been no word from Gavin, there was no change in her decision that she was doing the right thing and Ardith boarded the plane for California.

Ardith had chosen with exceptional care the outfit Gavin would see her in for the first time in months. It was a beautifully cut suit of natural slubbed silk, bought at the end of the season, but right for the cool coastal fall in Carmel. With it she wore a tailored turquoise silk blouse that deepened her extraordinary blue eyes. Her skin had a lovely apricot tinge from the summer at the beach.

Her hair, dark and lustrous, was drawn back and up in Gavin's favorite style and showed off the delicate opal earrings he had sent her from Australia. Her inner anticipation of their reunion shone in the dancing excitement of her eyes and a radiance about her whole person. Even the jet plane seemed to be traveling too slowly for her.

At the Monterey Airport Ardith debated whether to rent a car, use the limo service, or take a taxi over to Carmel. Deciding a taxi would be the least hassle, she opted for that and with an escalating heartbeat rode the short distance in a kind of dazed excitement.

After the driver had taken the bags out of the trunk and driven away, Ardith stood for a minute looking at the little chalet she had pictured so often in her daydreams of this moment.

A light was on in the upstairs window! *Gavin must already be here,* she thought, drawing a deep breath. She fumbled in her handbag for the key she had fingered so often in anticipation, and picking up her suitcases she went through the gate, over the rustic bridge, and up the steps to the front door.

With a hand that shook slightly Ardith fitted the key into the lock and turned it slowly, pushed the door open, and walked inside.

In the living room, a fire was glowing brightly in the tiled fireplace. Her heart was in her throat as she took a few steps farther into the high-ceilinged room.

"Gavin?" she said softly.

It was then she saw the tray on the coffee

table. There was a bottle of champagne cooling in a silver bucket of ice, and two glasses were chilling, stems up, beside it. Champagne? Perhaps Gavin had forgotten she did not drink champagne.

The unwanted memory of Renay's sarcasm thrust itself into Ardith's mind.

This was a special celebration. But Gavin knew — Ardith was momentarily distracted by the sight of a package alongside the tray. It was wrapped in glittering silver paper with a large shiny bow. Gavin had a present for her! Ardith was glad she had in her purse the monogrammed cuff links she had bought and wrapped for him. She started to pull the small box from her handbag when she heard footsteps above.

She turned quickly and went to the foot of the winding staircase.

"Gavin!" she called up hopefully.

The footsteps overhead quickened, and Ardith lifted her head expecting to see Gavin coming to the head of the steps.

But a moment later, to her puzzled dismay, she saw Renay instead!

The expression on Renay's face was hard to describe. It was a mixture of disbelief and anger; then it hardened into a cold disdain. "What are *you* doing here? Didn't you get Gavin's telegram telling you *not* to come?"

Ardith took a step back as if struck by a blow. Nausea churned in her stomach.

"What do you mean? Isn't Gavin here?" She looked up at Renay who seemed all at once in control again. Renay descended the steps, dressed in a sliver of a hostess gown, made of a shimmering material that slithered over her body. A knee-high slit showed a length of slender leg and delicate ankles in sling-back sandals.

"No, Gavin isn't here, at the moment. But I'm expecting him any time, as you can see," she said suggestively. "I certainly wasn't expecting *you*."

Ardith recoiled at the venom in Renay's voice.

"Gavin and I were supposed to meet here," she managed to say with stiff lips. "We planned before he left that we would —"

"Well, my dear, those plans have changed. It's really too bad you didn't get word. But you know Gavin, poor darling, procrastinated until the last minute, I guess, to send the telegram. It went to some place called Sunnyfields —"

"My grandmother's home," Ardith explained slowly, not yet grasping the situation. "I wasn't there. I was at my house at Seawood Beach."

Renay shrugged. "Well, I guess he didn't know. Anyway, I know he didn't want you to come."

"You mean — he's changed his mind about —" Ardith stammered unbelievingly. If he had — why was Renay here? It seemed a cruel way to tell her. Simply not meeting her would have been enough.

"I guess his irresponsible ways have backfired again! He should have written you from Melbourne. I kept telling him — but he kept putting it off. I guess he couldn't face telling you.

"You know what a coward he can be. Didn't he do this to you once before? That's Gavin. I told you he needs someone like me. Someone to do his dirty work for him, manage his *affairs*."

With an exaggerated sigh she went on. "Gavin's finally realized I'm the one he can depend on. He needs someone to lean on, and believe me, he's leaned heavily on me the last month."

Renay walked over to a table, opened the lid of a cigarette box, took one, and fitted it into her long holder. Then she turned to Ardith, who was rooted at the foot of the staircase. "It really is too bad you've come all this way for no reason. But, at least give him credit for *trying* to stop you. I can't imagine why you didn't get the telegram. They should have forwarded it —"

She lit her cigarette, inhaled, and blew out smoke daintily. Then with another little shrug she spoke in a pseudo-sympathetic tone. "I'm sure you'd rather avoid seeing Gavin now. It would be so embarrassing for you both." She moved over to the phone on the desk. "Shall I call you a cab? I'm sure you don't want to be here when Gavin arrives."

Gavin had told her this would be the longest foreign tour he had ever undertaken. And it was also the first time that Renay had accompanied him the whole length of the tour. That had been necessary because of the number of countries and the language problems. Also, since Renay had made all the initial contacts in each place, she was the one best qualified to see things went smoothly at each concert.

Was it possible that something new had developed in their relationship? Could it have changed — somehow — from a business one to a more personal, intimate one? It seemed improbable and yet —

Ardith looked again at the champagne, the gift-wrapped package, the firelight, the whole intimate atmosphere she had stumbled into. A rendezvous, obviously. But for whom?

Renay's hand was on the phone already. But there was something in her movement, a quick, almost apprehensive glance at the front door, that alerted Ardith, and when Renay repeated her suggestion that Ardith leave, Ardith said coolly, "I don't believe you, Renay. I think I'll stay. If Gavin doesn't want me here, he can tell me himself."

That seemed to startle Renay, but she maintained her self-control. "Why put yourself and Gavin through a scene that would only humiliate you? I've tried to spare you, but you don't want to believe Gavin is the man he is. You want him to be something you've dreamed up. Well, he isn't. Why not be gone when he comes? At least you'd have your pride!" Renay picked up the phone, and her long fingers with their polished nails poised above the dial.

Ardith clenched her jaw, fighting tears of rage and hurt. "My pride isn't at stake. I want to hear all this from Gavin."

Renay's mouth twisted as she struggled to confine her temper. Her voice was hard and cold. "As you like. But it may be a long wait. He was still in the city when he called me."

Ardith turned away and walked over to the window, staring blindly out into the darkening evening. Was Renay telling the truth? Could Gavin really have tried to stop her from coming? Was this the meaning of the long silence, the lack of letters, the almost total lack of communication the last six weeks? Was he really afraid to face her? Was Renay running interference for him as he himself had once told her she often did?

Ardith bit her lip as all the old scars reopened. Had Gavin betrayed her trust — *again?* Maybe Renay was right after all. Maybe even Gavin's story that Hans Friedborg had intercepted his mail had been a lie. Maybe this was his way of dealing with promises that became problems.

How could she have been such a fool to be taken in by his charm twice? *Didn't you learn anything in ten years?* Ardith suddenly demanded of herself.

As her mind began to add things up one after the other, her injured pride and assaulted ego surfaced. The humiliation that followed was deep and blinding.

Ardith whirled around, trembling, and said in a steely voice to Renay, "On second thought, go ahead and call that cab."

Ardith turned back to the window, hearing the whir of the dial as Renay made the call.

The wait seemed endless. The strain between the two women standing at opposite ends of the room stretched with sizzling tension. At last, there was the sound of a car outside. As Ardith quickly snatched up her purse and started toward the hallway, the front door burst open, and Gavin came in smiling.

But at the sight of Ardith, he halted. His face paled visibly. Shock replaced the smile. He glanced quickly at Renay, a glance that Ardith immediately interpreted as guilty.

"Ardith! What are you doing here? Didn't you get my telegram? I thought you — I didn't expect you!"

"Obviously," Ardith replied with all the calm she could summon. "Renay tells me you didn't want me to come. True or not?"

A muscle in Gavin's jaw tightened. He looked over at Renay as if to check. Then he nodded slowly. Of Renay he asked, "How much have you told her?"

"I tried to explain everything," Renay said smoothly. "She doesn't believe that you wanted it this way —"

Gavin started toward Ardith. "I thought

it would be better this way until I —"

But Ardith cut him off furiously. "Better or *easier?* I think you mean easier. It doesn't matter. I asked for the truth and I got it."

"But, that's not —"

"Oh, forget it!" she said angrily. "Don't bother with any excuses, any more explanations. Renay has made it all very clear. I understand now. My coming was a terrible mistake!"

Outside a car horn announced the arrival of the taxi.

Ardith threw Renay an ironic smile. "Perfect timing, right?" She started toward the door, brushing by a stunned Gavin. "Good-bye, Gavin. Good luck!"

"Ardith! No, wait —" she heard Gavin stammer as she went out the door. "Ardith! Where are you going? Wait! What did Renay say to you? Wait for me, Ardith —" His voice followed her out into the night.

But she was running down the steps, across the bridge, through the gate, and into the cab. "Hurry!" she half-sobbed to the driver. "Go! The Monterey Airport!"

With a grinding of gears, the cab jerked forward, away from the house and down the road.

Reaching the airport, Ardith found she was just in time to get on a commuter flight back to San Francisco. But in San Francisco she had to wait until ten o'clock for a flight east.

Numbed by shock, hurt beyond reason, Ardith remembered little of her night-long plane trip. All her illusions had been stripped from her, all her dreams and hopes of a new life, of a second chance to love and be loved. She closed her eyes and relived the ugly scene with Renay and the revealing one with Gavin. Everything in his looks or actions reinforced the suspicion Renay had already planted in Ardith's mind.

It was all too obvious that the two of them were planning an evening of celebration alone together at the little house she and Gavin were to have shared.

It was so cruel, so heartbreaking. Ardith huddled in the plane seat under the blanket the stewardess had brought her and shivered.

How long will it take me to get over Gavin this time? she moaned to herself.

Chapter Fourteen

When the plane touched down, Ardith rented a car and drove right to the beach house. She did not want to go to Sunnyfields or have her grandmother see her in her present state of mind. She drove through the night, arriving at dawn to see the outline of the cottage silhouetted against the gray-pink morning sky.

She fell into bed, exhausted, and slept until late afternoon, waking to a sulky, overcast sky and an ocean the color of lead.

She put on her jeans, pulled on a T-shirt, found her windbreaker and sneakers, and went out of the house down to the beach. The fog-damp air plastered her hair against her forehead and beaded her face. The surf was wild, the water as turbulent and dark as her feelings and thoughts.

The harsh, lonely cries of the sea gulls swooping overhead seemed to echo her own loneliness, her feeling of abandonment. She walked for a long time until, tired and chilled, she went back to the cottage.

Ardith made herself some tea, sitting hunched in front of the small wood-burning stove, trying to warm herself. Her mind was dense with pain.

Now that she was alone, her mind burned with new memories to torment her, new ones to forget. That week in San Francisco took its place along with Switzerland as a place of betrayal.

All her emotions were unchecked. Disillusionment and disappointment swept over her, so pervasive that all she could do was rock back and forth, longing to weep away the awful ache inside her.

She could not even pray. She did not even know how to pray or what to pray for. She remembered once hearing a minister say there were times in life when all one could do was cry, "Mercy!"

Ardith finally fell wearily into bed and went to sleep with the strong wind rattling the windows and the surf pounding so loudly it seemed to be crashing right up onto the front porch.

When she woke up the next morning, it was raining hard. She fixed herself some coffee. She felt physically better after the night's sleep.

She was glad she had come to the beach house. It was the place that had brought her through before. She had survived that dreadful time in her life, and she would survive this one, too. *With God's help,* she added prayerfully.

The day crawled by in a kind of empty, endless loneliness. The stormy rain continued, and the wind rose steadily all afternoon. Since Ardith had enough firewood to keep the little stove going, it was warm and dry inside the cottage.

She knew where she would find comfort and healing, and that afternoon she pulled out her Bible and read hungrily. In Luke 6, reading Jesus' admonition to forgive, Ardith stopped. She knew she would have to forgive Gavin — and Renay — before her broken heart could begin to heal. That was hard. But somehow she couldn't go on reading without doing it.

Ardith put down the Bible and slipped to her knees on the bare floor. Pressing her forehead into clasped hands she prayed.

She did not know how long she knelt there or how many times she said over and over, "I forgive them. Help me, Lord, to get rid of all these awful feelings against them, please! Help me to forgive fully."

When she finally rose to her feet, for the first time since she had left California, the awful heaviness and the tension in her throat and chest were lighter. Her mind was emptied, and in spite of the racket of the wind and rain that night, she slept soundly.

Toward dawn she was startled awake. The wind was blowing with a fury that seemed to shake the whole cottage.

It was frightening. Ardith had never been down here so late in the year, and she had forgotten that September was part of the hurricane season. She had stayed the week after Labor Day before and there had been hurricane alerts on the radio, savage storms sometimes, but always the predictions had come to nothing. The hurricanes had eventually blown out to sea.

But there seemed a difference about this one. Ardith got up and tried to look out through the rain-pelted windows. Maybe she should leave before she was stranded. As soon as it was light, she would pack up and drive to Sunnyfields.

Apprehensive, Ardith switched on the small transistor radio to see if she could get a weather report. To her alarm, she found an emergency warning and it was repeated five minutes later. A tropical storm was turning into a full-blown hurricane. "Anyone living in the following areas should evacuate immediately!" Seawood

Beach was among those areas.

She got dressed, packed up the few groceries left on the shelves, and waited tensely for the first signs of day.

Then, above the roar of the wind and the battering sound of the surf, Ardith heard a car pull up outside and the slam of a door. Heavy footsteps on the wooden porch, and a ferocious knock at the door confirmed that someone, a man, had driven up.

It was probably a state trooper or someone from the Coast Guard station checking to see that the occupant had been alerted to leave the area.

Ardith hurried to answer and tell him she was ready to go at first light. But when she opened the door the man in a slicker was neither a trooper nor a Coast Guardsman — it was Gavin!

"What are *you* doing here?" she gasped.

"I've come to get you out of here before the roads are completely impassable," he said. "Get your things. We've got to hurry!"

"But — how —"

"Don't wait to ask questions. I'll explain everything. I've been at Sunnyfields. I was frantic to find you, and your grandmother said you were probably down here. Then when we heard about the storm, the possible hurricane . . . She's out of her mind with worry about you. Come on!" He took hold of Ardith's arm.

She resisted. "I've got a car — a rental. I can drive myself."

"Leave it! It's under the carport. It will be okay! Besides those companies have insurance.

"Ardith! There's no time to argue. Anyway, we've got to talk! And besides, I told your grandmother I'd take care of you, bring you home safely." Gavin was adamant.

In spite of her shock and mixed feelings at seeing Gavin, here, Ardith was aware of the danger and knew it would be foolhardy to refuse to go with him. Explanations could come later. She pulled on her windbreaker, grabbed her handbag, and quickly gathered up the things she had ready. With Gavin's arm sheltering her against the fierce driving force of the storm, they went outside to her grandmother's station wagon.

It was slow driving to Sunnyfields. The roads were clogged with other late-season tourists, cottage dwellers, and vacationers trying to get home to safety. Many of the roads were flooded and they had to detour.

At these times and places Gavin began

to talk to Ardith, slowly unraveling the mystery of what had happened in Carmel and all that had led up to that terrible moment of misunderstanding.

"I did send a telegram telling you not to come — but it said not to come on the *tenth*. I only wanted a few days' delay until I knew — the results of something I was waiting for." He fumbled in the pocket of his jacket under the mackintosh and handed her a crumpled yellow envelope. "At least I wrote out the message for Renay to send. It was sent to Sunnyfields. I assumed you'd be there."

Ardith tore open the envelope and smoothed out the wrinkled telegram. "You sent this?" she said. Then she read, " 'Plans changed. Do not come to Carmel on the tenth. I am no longer free to meet you. Gavin Parrish.' "

Gavin jerked his head so quickly the car swerved sightly. Then he hit the steering wheel with his fist. "That's not the message I wanted sent! Renay altered the wording herself." He shook his head. "Believe me, Ardith. There was more to it than that. I didn't want you not to come at all — as that implies — I just wanted to delay your arrival for a good reason. No wonder you got the wrong idea —"

"But even though I didn't get the telegram, when I got to Carmel, Renay led me to believe —"

"*Renay!* Let me tell you about Renay! No! That's a whole other story. It wasn't all her fault. I gave her much too much power over my life. She felt she had created me — at least, my public image. Unfortunately, she also began trying to control my private life."

He gave a harsh laugh. "Would you believe she even managed my interviews for me? She presumed the right to edit, like that piece in *Celebrity* magazine — I hope you didn't see it!"

Not waiting for an answer, he went on. "Renay had some crazy idea that if you were out of the picture — she and I — oh, it's ridiculous, I never thought of her like that. She was a good manager-agent, tough-minded and efficient, but I let her take over so much of my life she thought she could program this part as well."

"But what *is* the reason you didn't want me to come as we had planned?" persisted Ardith, still finding it hard to believe she and Gavin were driving together through a storm-battered area on their way to Sunnyfields. She had thought it was all over.

"Well, I can tell you now," he sighed. "But I was afraid — I wanted to double-check at Stanford Medical Center when I got back to California."

"Stanford Medical Center — what do you mean? Are you ill?"

"No, thank God. And I *mean* that, *thank God!* But, when I was on tour, I began to have problems with my hands, numbness, stiffness in the finger joints. I went into a panic before each concert, afraid I might stumble, miss notes, not be able to reach octaves. It got so bad I finally had to see a doctor. Actually, a number of doctors.

"We had to cancel a few concerts. They put me in the hospital and ran dozens of tests, scans — all sorts of unpleasant and terrifying tests. I find I'm not a very good patient. Then there was all the waiting for the results to see what was going on. It was a nightmare.

"At any rate, although they don't have a name for it, they finally decided it wasn't some deteriorating disease like muscular dystrophy or multiple sclerosis."

"Oh, Gavin, how awful! But why didn't you tell me? Why didn't you write?" asked Ardith.

"For one thing, it became difficult for me to use my hands at all, especially the right one. Then I was hesitant to alarm you. It might have been just something psychosomatic or my imagination.

"I'm sorry, my darling. I kept thinking it would clear up or — Forgive me?"

"Yes, of course, but what happened then?" Now that her prayers had freed her of her jealousy, she found forgiveness easier.

"Well, even though the doctors in Australia gave me a clean bill of health, saying that with rest my hands would gradually improve and I would get back their full use, I wanted to get a second and definite okay from the doctors in the States. That's why I sent the telegram for you to delay coming. I wanted to be absolutely sure you wouldn't be marrying an invalid of some sort —"

"But, Gavin, when you marry, you marry 'in sickness and in health,' " Ardith reminded him gently.

"That might have been all right if it had happened after our vows, but I couldn't let you in for something like that if I knew beforehand."

After trying to absorb all this for a long moment, Ardith then asked Gavin another question, the one she had pondered over and over.

"But why was Renay waiting for you at the house in Carmel? When I walked in it was the perfect scene for a romantic rendezvous — presents, firelight, champagne for two. She was wearing — well, she looked as if she were expecting her lover —"

"That was all her doing, believe me, darling!" Gavin said earnestly. "You see, I checked into the hospital right from the airport. I asked her to open the house, get in supplies, and see that it was aired and ready for — *us!*"

"Still — she implied you had called her from the city and were coming down to be there with her."

"I did call her from the city, told her everything was negative — the tests, I mean. The champagne was her way of celebrating the good news. In fact, the one thing I did learn about my paralysis is that it seems to recur whenever I learn that Renay has intruded on my plans. As my tension level goes up, my fingers lose their flexibility."

He sighed. "The rest you know. As soon as I'd realized exactly what had happened, I got the next available flight out of San Francisco for North Carolina."

Three hours later they were welcomed back to Sunnyfields by a grateful Charlotte.

The next morning, after a good night's sleep and a hearty breakfast, Gavin and Ardith, their arms about each other's waist, wandered along the orchard path where rosy apples were ripening on the old trees.

The autumn sun slanted through the arched trellis and threw latticed patterns on the wooden table where they sat down across from each other. They still had not had time to say all the things in their hearts.

"After all that's happened, we are really here together," Ardith sighed.

"I'm not sure I'll ever be able to tell you how much I love you," Gavin said earnestly, taking both her hands in his. "How thankful I am to have found you again. I'm going to spend the rest of my life proving to you that you haven't misplaced your love and trust."

"I know, Gavin. And I want to be the kind of wife you will always feel that way about."

"I want to tell you something else, Ardith, something very important. Those days when I was lying in the hospital bed in Australia, not knowing what lay ahead of me, I did some hard, serious thinking and —" He paused.

There was a tremor in his voice, and

Ardith looked at him in puzzled surprise. She had never seen Gavin display this kind of emotion.

"— and I recommitted my life to Christ. I just said, 'Whatever happens I want to give it all to you. Whatever is your will for my life, Lord, that's what I want, too.' "

Ardith was suddenly overcome by a deep thankfulness and a rush of joy. She recognized the new light in Gavin's loving eyes.

Her heart was too full for words. But there was, after all, no need for them. Gavin leaned across the table and kissed her, a kiss sweet with tender promise.

Ardith's eyes glistened with tears as she thought, *Surely, the Lord HAS watched between Gavin and me while we were absent from one another.*

And now he was harmonizing the discordant notes of both their lives into a symphony of faith, hope, and love.

The employees of Thorndike Press hope you have enjoyed this Large Print book. All our Thorndike and Wheeler Large Print titles are designed for easy reading, and all our books are made to last. Other Thorndike Press Large Print books are available at your library, through selected bookstores, or directly from us.

For information about titles, please call:

(800) 223-1244

or visit our Web site at:

www.gale.com/thorndike
www.gale.com/wheeler

To share your comments, please write:

Publisher
Thorndike Press
295 Kennedy Memorial Drive
Waterville, ME 04901